The
Migration
of Butterflies

OTHER BOOKS BY CAROL MALYON

FICTION

The Adultery Handbook
Mixed-up Grandmas *(for children)*
Lovers & Other Strangers
If I Knew I'd Tell You
The Edge of the World

POETRY

Colville's People
Emma's Dead
Headstand

The
Migration
of Butterflies

A Novel by Carol Malyon

THE MERCURY PRESS

The publisher gratefully acknowledges the financial assistance of the Canada Council for the Arts, the Ontario Arts Council, the Ontario Media Development Corporation, and the Ontario Book Publishing Tax Credit Program. The publisher further acknowledges the financial support of the Government of Canada through the Department of Canadian Heritage's Book Publishing Industry Development Program (BPIDP) for our publishing activities.

Editor: Beverley Daurio
Cover, composition and page design: Beverley Daurio
Cover painting: *Motif in Orange* (2004) by Holly Briesmaster

Printed and bound in Canada
Printed on acid-free paper

1 2 3 4 5   08 07 06 05 04

Library and Archives Canada Cataloguing in Publication

Malyon, Carol, 1933–
The migration of butterflies / Carol Malyon.
ISBN 1-55128-111-2
I. Title.
PS8576.A5364M53 2004   C813'.54   C2004-905904-1

The Mercury Press
Box 672, Station P, Toronto, Ontario Canada M5S 2Y4
www.themercurypress.ca

I have the best kids in the world.
This book is for them.

Now the once worm soars
over mountain trees on whose leaves
it had one-time crawled.

Fred Cogswell

I do not know whether I was then a man dreaming I was
a butterfly, or whether I am now a butterfly, dreaming
I am a man.

Chuangtse

i remembr th stars falling
                              in our arms th nite yu
    found me
              in madagaskar
                              i remembr our wings
    falling off

bill bissett

1998

Summer

Nancy turns photo album pages slowly, awkwardly, because she's holding a toddler on her lap. 'Long ago,' she says, 'there was another baby named Fern. Here she is, being pushed in a big carriage, the kind they used in the old days. Isn't it fancy? It's made of wicker, like the chairs on Grandma's verandah. And here's a picture when she was a little girl like you, building sand castles on a beach. See. She has a pail and shovel like yours. Now look, she's grown up into a teenager reading a book on a park bench. See her standing outside a church? She's getting married. That's why she's wearing that pretty white dress. Here she is again with her husband and two little girls. Pay attention. Watch what happens in these pictures. She keeps growing older and older.'

'Hey, there's you!'

'That's right. Fern and I are waiting at an airport to take a ride on a little plane. Someday you and I will fly on a plane like that. We'll fly up into the sky like a bird or butterfly. When we look down we'll see the roofs of houses and the tops of trees. Roads will be so far away that they'll look like pencil lines on a piece of paper. Here's a picture of the ferry boat that took us to the airport.'

'Will the fairies come on our plane ride?'

'Hmmm?'

'You said it was a fairy boat.'

'Oh. Not that kind of fairy. I meant...'

'What's that big thing?'

'A grain elevator down by the lake. It's a very tall building for storing some kind of grain. Maybe wheat, for baking bread. I'm not sure whether it's still there.'

'It's too big. It couldn't move.'

'That's right, sweetie. But sometimes, if a building is falling apart or isn't needed any more, it gets knocked down. The broken pieces are taken away, and something else is built there instead. Old things get replaced.'

'What's this paper with lots of writing?'

'Some bible words Fern and I liked.'

'Tell me.'

'Well, okay, but they're hard words. You won't understand them... *whither thou goest, I will go: and where thou lodgest, I will lodge: thy people shall be...*'

'Okay. Stop now! I don't like those words.'

'It just means that people who love each other try to stay together. Fern and I loved each other, and we stayed together as long as we could.'

'Where is she?'

'Fern was very old. Her time was over. She died before you were born.'

'Did you cry?'

'I cried a lot. I loved Fern and missed her so much. But Fern knew she was going to die soon, and she was ready to have it happen.'

'I want to see her.'

'She wanted to see you too. But she was too old and couldn't wait. We have all these pictures to look at instead.' Nancy riffles through the pages again. 'This is the way life is,' she says. 'This is how our lives happen. We start out as little babies, and then keep growing older. Someday I'll be an old woman like Fern, but not for a long long time. Not until after you've grown up. Someday you'll grow old too.'

'Bye, old lady.' The toddler slams the photo album shut. 'C'mon, Momma. Let's play airplane. I steer. You're the old lady who wants a ride.'

1995

August

BATHURST QUAY

Butterflies migrate to Mexico, to California. Perhaps first they'll gather on trees at Bathurst Quay.

Planes travel beyond the point of no return. So do we all: butterflies and people. These women: Fern, Nancy, Sarah.

It is August. Changes are taking place.

Along the lake the early morning mist is beginning to disappear. Three grey figures emerge from the gloom. Wavering strangers. Perhaps they'll see each other, perhaps they'll speak.

FERN: GNAWING MEMORIES INSTEAD OF BREAKFAST

'What's the matter? Are you deaf?' Fern reaches up with her cane and yanks at the signal cord again and again: ding ding ding ding ding. 'Stop this infernal trolley! I want to get off right here!'

'Yeah, lady. I heard you the first time. Hold your horses. Wait'll we get around the corner.'

Once the streetcar comes to a complete stop Fern struggles up from her seat. She is slow, awkward, her joints stiffened up again. She grabs the railing tight, then clambers down the steps, steadying herself, reaching her good leg down first, then the other.

The doors jerk shut behind her. Fern shakes her cane at the driver as he pulls away. 'I wanted to get off back at the corner,' she hollers. As if he cares, she thinks. Of course not. Why should he? As if I care about him either.

Fern looks around. She's not even on the curb. She is standing on a safety island, a shelf of concrete out in the middle of Fleet Street. 'What a stupid place to let me off,' she mutters, then looks up, notices a sign above her head, fastened to the pole she's been leaning against, STREETCAR STOP. Stupid bureaucrats, she thinks, stupid politicians. What a bunch of ignorant dingbats. Always interfering. Changing whatever's perfectly good in the first place. Trying to pretend they're efficient. Fiddling with busy-work. Better they should take up knitting or just sit and twiddle their thumbs, keep out of mischief.

Fern grumbling like always, muttering, fed up. Everything's deteriorating. This old century's almost over, worn out, used-up. It'll soon be gone. Good riddance, she thinks. It's high time.

She walks back to the sidewalk at the corner of Bathurst and Fleet Streets, and stands on the curb, right by the spot where the streetcar stop used to be, then leans on her cane and looks around.

That Loblaws warehouse on the north-east corner, it's pretty beat-up looking now, some windows broken, and the big Loblaws sign is gone. Fern crosses over to take a look, sees a food bank sign instead. That's okay. People can't get along without food. What? No bread? So feed them cake. Who said that? Someone beheaded. Marie Antoinette, maybe. Or that woman who kept on knitting. Someone who'd never been hungry in her whole life.

Fern stares at the south-east corner next. That nice old Crosse & Blackwell building. Some other name is probably on it now, she's too far away to read what it says. A famous architect designed the place, someone important, who was it? The name's on the tip of her tongue. Don't swallow, she thinks. An old chestnut, but she laughs anyway, wheezes a bit, then laughs again. She ought to be able to remember his name. He designed lots of important places: the Sunnyside pool maybe, or the Princes' Gate at the exhibition grounds. Isn't there some story about that Crosse & Blackwell building, hidden somewhere, locked in some back cupboard of her brain? Maybe. Anyway, so what? She doesn't need it. Leave it alone. Let it stay put and gather dust.

But look there, beyond the building, a faint outline against the sky. So beautiful, oh just look, the old grain silo for Canada Malting. Once she drove across the prairies. She remembers seeing grain elevators outlined against the empty sky, shimmering in the distance, alive, beckoning.

But this silo seems so puny, smaller than she remembers, maybe because so many tall buildings in Toronto have surpassed it. Especially that CN Tower, the tallest, what is it? structure somewhere, in the world maybe, or North America at least.

Fern peers south-west now, can almost see the glass windows of Tip Top Tailors waver in and out of focus through her milky cataracts and the morning mist.

Nothing else she remembers. Everything's gone, gone, all gone. The round Maple Leaf Baseball Stadium: gone. The cute little Joy gas station shaped like a child's castle: gone. And Little Norway, dear Little Norway. Nothing of it remains. The chain-link fence, the sentry box at the entrance, all the barracks buildings: gone, all of them gone. She already knew this, of course, has been down here before, but all the same it would have been lovely to see them again. Nothing left but murky memories. Fern scrunches her eyes shut, tries to imagine Little Norway back into place. She wishes she had some snapshots. They might help.

The lake is still there. Busy-work politicians couldn't get rid of that, bulldoze it away to some different place. Fern heads toward it.

She walks south, slowly, stopping to rest every few steps, ignoring the red light, and the words lit up beneath it, DON'T WALK. It is early in the morning, six a.m. maybe, almost no traffic, but it doesn't matter: Fern would ignore the warning signal anyway. She is sorting out jigsaw puzzle pieces of her past, and it takes all her attention. The light changes from red to green, then back to red again before she gets all the way across.

There are no pedestrians around, but if there were and they looked closely, Fern knows what they'd see. Nothing much. A skinny old woman with short white hair, maybe still tangled from sleep. Did she comb it before she left home? She can't remember. Wearing a flowered skirt and flowered top that will probably clash when the sun comes up. A red canvas bag slung over her shoulder, wooden cane clutched tight in her hand. Wearing high-top running shoes with orange fluorescent laces from a carton found in a laundromat. A sign said, 'Help yourself,' and so Fern did. She had to, they seemed so sporty and alive. From a distance strangers would only see her outline, and maybe her flashy shoelaces which holler: hey! Look over here! Pay attention! Guess what! I'm still alive!

Her daughters hate them. Well, of course.

The shoes don't quite fit though. Fern's feet hurt already. She shuffles slowly along Queen's Quay, glaring at all the newer build-ings. She hadn't expected apartments. Not here at Bathurst Quay, the old Fleet Street Flats. She sees a playing field to the south. That's more like it. She remembers games at the old Maple Leaf Stadium. If she squeezes her eyes shut, she can almost see a ball game begin to happen, almost hear the cheering crowd. There'd be popcorn and hot dogs. She feels hungry, her stomach rumbling, loud as a trolley. Well, no wonder. That's what she gets for sneaking out early, with-out breakfast, quick, before Ruby woke up. Too late now to think about food.

Fern finds flags, peers at the historic plaques beneath them, but it's still too dark to read, if she has even remembered to bring her glasses. This place feels like a deserted graveyard. She bumps against a park bench. Good. She flops down to rest.

NANCY: ON THE MOVE, AROUND-THE-CLOCK

A young woman has a transit pass and can travel anywhere, which suits her fine; that's where she's going. It's been three days now. Sometimes she rides all-night streetcars and buses until the subway stations open again. Perhaps she gets off at a donut shop and buys coffee and day-old muffins, lingering as long as she can, reading all the newspapers left behind on the sticky tables. She doesn't do this very often; she can't afford it.

In the daytime she visits one library after another, opens a few books at a study carrel, then rests her head on her arms and falls asleep.

She is nineteen years old and wears spiky cyan hair, fake leather clothes. Men pay attention.

She has given up smoking, but cigarettes are still on her mind, and Brad is on her mind and his child is in her belly.

Bus drivers make conversation: 'Kinda late to be out, eh? Just getting home?' When she gets off they warn, 'Look after yourself. Be careful now.' Sometimes they ask what she's reading. She carries a book on butterflies that she bought at a yard sale for no reason. Now she leafs through it to find a baby name.

The words are beautiful. They flit around the blue sky of her mind:

Crescent

Painted Lady

Red-banded Hairstreak

Copper

Skipper

Sulphur

Zebra

Azure

Fritillary

Tortoise-shell

'Fritillary.' Nancy repeats and repeats it, liking the sound. But it would be too hard for a child to spell. She has trouble spelling the word herself. Skipper, maybe. Nancy smiles, imagining a little girl skipping along a sidewalk. But no. The name reminds her of Barbie dolls.

Or she might name the baby after the signs on buses and streetcars: Victoria, Wellesley, Neville, Jane. It is a heavy responsibility to pick out a perfect name.

She's not afraid to raise a child, not yet, though maybe she will be later on, when she's had more time to think about it, but she is terrified of the birth itself, of pain, of losing control. If the infant hears her screaming it will begin life shrieking too. She wants her baby to find this world a warm comforting happy place, but doesn't know how to make this happen.

Nancy wanders around the empty exhibition grounds and looks at silhouettes of buildings. She calls, 'Hiya, angel,' to the figure on top of the Princes' Gate, 'Got a pretty good view from up there? How ya doing? Have a nice day.' On a park bench in the middle of lush wet grass she dozes for a while.

A road leads down to the water, then turns and passes by yacht clubs: Alexandra, National. Alexandra is a princess name. A girl-baby would probably like it. Alexander for a boy.

Nancy daydreams: she brings Alexandra down here on the streetcar. They carry a picnic basket and fishing pole, the nice old-fashioned bamboo kind, like in a story about Tom Sawyer or Huckleberry Finn. Alexandra dangles a line into the lake and never catches anything, she doesn't want to, doesn't use a hook. She just wants to dangle her line in the sparkling water while sailboats drift like ripples past her eyes, while seagulls glide up and down the dazzling sky. Alexandra's mother watches her every minute and her eyes are full of love.

Of course her mother makes sure Alexandra is wearing sunscreen, whichever one gives the best protection.

The sign at a yacht club parking lot prohibits this and that. No non-members. Alexandra and her mother don't want to go inside a stuffy building anyway. They wander on past holding hands. Maybe they skip along for a while, or run, or spin in circles. What do they care about parking lots? They don't own a car, don't even want one. They ride on buses and streetcars, a window wide-open beside them so the wind can get tangled inside their hair.

The concrete walkway goes nowhere. Nancy turns around.

SARAH: SCENTED GARDEN, METAL MAZE

It is Friday now, finally Friday, early morning, the second week in August. Has she slept yet? Sarah isn't sure. It's going to be another scorcher, the air already heavy and humid. Sarah takes a deep breath and nearly chokes.

She lies on an air mattress on her apartment balcony and sees everything that happens. Nothing happens.

But no. That's not true. Someone shuffles through Little Norway Park, heading toward the fragrant garden. Sarah closes her eyes and concentrates, tries to remember all the plants, the names printed on metal markers, dots raised in Braille designs. Allspice. Lavender. Beebalm. Lamb's Ear. Mint. That's enough for now. Maybe she'll remember the others later.

Perhaps the person will wander through the metal maze in the playground, back and forth, back and forth. Sarah tries to imagine what this would look like. She has never seen anyone use it, not even a child. Perhaps this is the sort of magic that only happens in early morning.

Sarah opens her eyes again. A young woman walks along the street, her footsteps thumping, lub dub, a heart beat, a metronome.

The balcony faces south, toward the western gap, the island airport. She knows they are there, though it's too dark to see them. Sarah wishes she was in a highrise, could see beyond the island. At daybreak she could gaze at the endless blue shadings of Lake Ontario, unfocus her eyes and let the view soothe them. Like eye drops, she thinks, and then wonders, do they still make Murine drops? In the same small blue bottle? She thinks it was a wonderful marketing ploy. People probably bought them just to own that tiny bottle, deep blue as the depths of the Mediterranean Sea. Or is she thinking of ear drops? Auralgan, in a blue bottle. Beautiful word. 'Auralgan.' She repeats it like a mantra, 'O ral gan, o ral gan,' hoping the sound will lull her back to sleep. It doesn't work.

Sarah watches windows in nearby apartments, as they come alive, one after another, yellow squares of light. They remind her as always of a Hopper painting.

The street is deserted again. She hears the mournful horn on the airport ferry. It will sound again in fifteen minutes. Soon she'll be sitting on the concrete steps at the water-taxi landing. She will sip at her mug of coffee and watch the ferry move back and forth, carrying people who also intend to travel.

She makes a mental note to pack her binoculars. You never know. She might need them.

Sarah gets up, she might as well, and goes inside to take a shower.

FERN WAVES AT PEOPLE WHO DON'T WAVE BACK

Fern sits on a concrete step. Below her other steps descend into the water, green seaweed clinging to them, flowing back and forth like mermaid hair. Her running shoes have been tossed behind her, orange shoelaces still knotted. Beside them a red sock and a purple one, both inside out.

Fern's feet are in the water. She wiggles her toes, staring at them, as though they belong to someone else. 'Toes.' She says the word aloud for no reason. Her toes glow beneath the water, like white grubs emerging from beneath a lush suburban lawn. When she and Walter lived in the suburbs it was always important to grow a good lawn.

Planes take off across the gap. It doesn't matter where they're going. Fern wishes she could go along.

The ferry is leaving without her too. Fern waves her cane at passengers who don't wave back. She shakes it again. The passengers still ignore her so she heaves her cane at them as hard as she can. It floats for a moment just beyond her reach, then disappears beneath the surface. 'Good riddance,' she mutters.

Perhaps the passengers couldn't see her, she thinks. Perhaps she's invisible, and only dreams this. A fantasy of sitting on concrete steps and dabbling her bare feet in water, wriggling her white arthritic toes. That dream.

Long ago in some old magazine, she read of a Chinese philosopher who believed he turned into a butterfly each night. He kept wondering: am I a man dreaming I'm a butterfly, or am I a butterfly dreaming I'm a man? In *Reader's Digest* maybe. It's the kind of story they might print.

Fern likes to daydream about that old question. Like now. She lets her mind loose, to wander in that direction: I wiggle my toes in the water. Is this the dream or the awake part? But anyway, what does it matter? My feet are free and so am I. The water is beautiful and cool and feels good. Nothing else matters. Not right now.

Turning into a butterfly: she tries to imagine what that would be like. A little caterpillar drifts off to sleep, wakes up days later, suddenly realizing that somehow it now has wings. Thinking I must be dreaming, but trying to move the wings up and down anyway. Yes! They really work! I can fly! No more of that humdrum old earthbound existence, inching along, struggling up the stiff stems of milkweed plants, stretching out again and again to reach and munch the bitter leaves, sometimes falling off, thwacking the ground, struggling to climb up the stem again.

Magical, miraculous. Suddenly soaring like a heavenly angel above puny people who are fastened like toadstools to the ground. If such a thing ever happened to me, Fern thinks, I would finally, absolutely, believe in God.

She sees a reflection on the water, someone standing beside her. Fern kicks her feet and the person shatters into little pieces. She considers whether to look up.

SUNGLASSES: A MIRRORED MASK TO HIDE BEHIND

Dammit. An old woman sits on the concrete steps, her bare feet dangling in the water. Sarah can hardly believe it.

The steps are always deserted and Sarah thinks of them as her own. This is where she sits with a coffee every weekend morning watching sailboats and planes drift through water and sky. Sarah can relax and close her eyes whenever she wants to, knowing they can manage without her. She doesn't have to take responsibility for them.

Today is Friday though, and all her duties have been abandoned.

'Who are you?' she asks the old woman. 'Are you all right?'

The old woman doesn't answer. She stares at her distorted feet rippling inside the water, and mumbles something.

'Once when I was a butterfly...'

Can that really be what she said? Sarah tries again. 'Do you live around here?'

'Fern.'

'Ferns? You're looking for ferns?' Sarah looks around and sees a few weeds: Queen Anne's Lace, daisies, plantain, yarrow. 'Sorry. Try some place else. No ferns around here.'

The ferry sounds its horn and the old woman waves. Oh for heaven's sake, thinks Sarah, don't draw attention. Just put your shoes on and go away and leave me alone. Surely it's not too much to ask.

'It's a name,' says the old woman. 'A plant, but also a name. Fern. What happened to all those nice Norwegian boys?'

Sarah checks the woman's wrists, looking for a plastic identification bracelet, in case she's wandered away from a hospital or nursing home. Nothing. She's just some ordinary old lady who's lost her marbles, Sarah thinks. A fruitcake, a nut case.

Lucky for Sarah that her mirror sunglasses are in her pocket. She can watch the old woman without her knowing. She can wait here on this bench until the old woman wanders away. There's no rush. Sarah opens her newspaper to the crossword puzzle. She places the want-ad section on the bench beside her. Someone else can have it. Her next job won't be in Toronto.

People will be startled when she doesn't show up for work, she's such a perfect worker, always on time, not chattering on the phone, never flirting in elevators and hallways. They'll be surprised, but no one will panic. No department head will call to ask about some overdue file. The bitchy green-fingernails supervisor might notify Personnel. Someone will probably phone her at home and leave a message on the machine. But they won't be concerned. Not until Monday.

Sarah imagines them finally checking her desk some time next week. Looking through the files on top of her desk, one after another, finding everything complete. Finally realizing what a treasure she is. Repeating, 'Wow! Isn't that amazing!'

Someone opening the desk drawers, discovering all her personal belongings gone. Only a single piece of paper, neatly typed, 'Fuck you! Fuck you all!' Their names listed below, Martin not heading the list, simply filed alphabetically, lost in the middle. Inconsequential. She wishes she could see their faces: the pinched green-talons supervisor, Loreen, the pregnant girl from the mail room... Everyone twittering. Someone phoning Martin's department to tell him.

That old woman dabbling her feet in the water. What was it she said? 'Once I was a butterfly...' She must be crazy. What a nice idea though, being a butterfly. Sarah drifts off into a butterfly dream:

A beautiful creature hides inside a chrysalis, waiting to be reborn. Whatever mistakes it has made in life will be erased. Other creatures have been searching everywhere, wondering where the caterpillar could have gone. The butterfly slowly emerges, and shivers against the air; it had almost forgotten what air felt like. It unfolds its wings, moves them slowly up and down, drying them, practising for flight. People gaze in admiration. 'Oh look! It's so beautiful!' they keep saying. The butterfly ignores them, flutters above their heads and out of sight. They keep watching for a while, hoping it might return.

They'll keep dialing all day Monday, leaving messages that will never be answered. On Tuesday the phone will be disconnected. People will always wonder where she went.

THE EARTH KEEPS TURNING; OLD JOINTS CREAK

Fern glances behind her. That snoopy woman has moved to a park bench. Good riddance. The earth turns and people move on. The woman is wearing mirror sunglasses and her eyes are either open or else they're shut. She holds a newspaper as though she's reading, but surely she can't read through those mirrors. The woman must be faking.

Fern's knees creak whenever she moves them. Can the mirror-sunglasses woman hear them? Is she asleep? Will the creaking disturb her? Tough luck if it does. Move somewhere else then, Fern thinks, shoo, scram, skedaddle, leave me alone. Or maybe she says the words aloud.

BABIES

Sarah is hidden behind her newspaper and mirror sunglasses, lost inside a recent memory: Monday, only four days ago. As she walked along the waterfront on her way to work, mist was rising from the ground in Little Norway Park, lifting upward past the totem pole and flags and trees, blending into the grey sky.

But once she was east of the park it cleared. She stopped by a chain-link fence to admire a lovely untended landscape. Amid chunks of concrete, almost hidden by long grass, Queen Anne's lace and blue chicory. A Monet painting, a dappling of blue and green and white. A pale butterfly fluttered to and fro, then settled on a blossom of Queen Anne's lace. Sarah had wished she was a painter and could capture it on canvas, or at least had a camera handy. She lingered awhile, but finally had to look away. She felt like crying. Why? she wondered. Because of the beauty? Chicory and Queen Anne's lace keep reappearing every year, like a promise that life goes on, keeps renewing.

But it's a lie. Sarah gave her baby up for adoption years ago, and assumed she'd have another child later on, when she was ready, but it didn't happen.

A crew was working overhead on the Gardiner Expressway. Sarah looked up, watched as clouds of dust lifted up and then settled again inside the grey sky, like clouds of chalk dust from blackboard brushes. For a moment she remembered being a child, in a cinder schoolyard, banging brushes against each other to clean them. A little goody-goody, teacher's pet. The chalk dust seemed ominous somehow... But then Sarah glanced at her watch and hurried on so she wouldn't be late for work.

Only four days ago when life was beautiful. When Sarah still lived with Martin, slept with him, believed him. At coffee break that day she learned the young girl in the mail room was pregnant. At night Martin told her who the father was.

'Get out,' she hollered. 'Just get out.'

'Sarah, baby, it was a mistake. A stupid fling, a one-night stand. I was sorry the moment it happened.'

She grabbed her sewing scissors. 'Pack your clothes or I start cutting them up.'

'Don't be crazy,' Martin said, but he backed away, grabbed a suitcase.

Sarah looks up and notices a second person is sitting on the steps, a young woman with blue spiked hair. Perhaps she has come to take the older one home. But no, dammit. She is taking her shoes off too, her feet are sliding into the water.

FLOWER CHILDREN

Fern wakes up, notices a young woman sitting beside her. 'Willie?' she asks. 'Winnie?' then, 'No. Of course not. No.'

'Nancy.'

Fern glares. 'Who are you? Someone from social work? A public health nurse?'

'No. Relax. I'm no one. Just Nancy. Who are you?'

'Fern.'

'Wow. A flower-child name, like from the sixties.'

'Those long-hair hippies,' Fern scoffs. 'Woodstock. I'd already been alive a million years before folk songs with lots of verses, before peace signs and all those posters, MAKE LOVE NOT WAR. Those young people were so innocent and stupid. They smoked their marijuana cigarettes and the drug made them dream they could change the world.' She leans over, smacks her hands against the water. Drops of water fly into the sky. She smacks harder, soaking her blouse, soaking her skirt.

Soaking someone named Nancy who hollers, 'Hey!' then splashes back.

Nancy chews a piece of grass. 'This used to be water.'

Fern splashes again. 'It still is.'

'No, I mean this park where we're sitting, and the space behind us. The land the apartments were built on. All the way up to Fleet Street. The city filled it in.'

'No. I'm old. I'd remember.'

'It's true,' Nancy insists. 'I read about it in a book. I guess you're not old enough. How old are you anyway?'

Fern can't remember. 'None of your dratted business,' she says. This spy, Fern thinks, this snoopy girl who says her name is Nancy, who dabbles her feet in the water as though she's human. She's just another do-gooder, a busybody, a snoop; she's a spy from social work after all.

USED FURNITURE

Sarah wanders back to her apartment, to her round teacup balcony and waits for the two women to leave her favourite spot. This is her last day to enjoy it. They don't know this of course, and wouldn't care if they did. Of course not. Why should they? Sarah watches the world from her tiny balcony but isn't happy about it. She prefers sitting beside the water-taxi landing, day-dreaming, imagining the kind of dramas that might bring people to that place. A Ward's Island resident with a sudden emergency: an asthmatic child maybe, or a woman in labour, a man with chest pain radiating down his left arm and up into his jaw. Or simply a young couple who escaped their schools, their parents, their summer jobs. Visiting the island, moving beyond Toronto time. Explorers of the island and each other. Late at night, in the aftermath of that urgency called love. The last ferry has already left. The young couple walks slowly, their arms twined around each other like ivy. Time got away from them; it does that. Their clothes are rumpled and grass-stained and smell of fucking. They pooled their coins to pay for a water taxi to the mainland, but now all their money is gone. They sit on the concrete steps awhile, then finally begin the long walk home.

Sarah watches the women sitting at the water's edge, hunched over, appearing almost conspiratorial. Their arms are moving, as though they're splashing each other like little children.

Once she held a child inside her belly. Pain and misery for nine months and a lot more at the end. She wanted to hold the baby in her arms just once before it was taken away, but everyone knew better, her mother, the nurses, the Children's Aid worker. 'No,' they said, 'definitely not.' Knowing if she ever held it in her arms she'd just hold it, hold it, hold it, already loving it, protective, instantly maternal, refusing to ever let go.

She had assumed she'd have another, of course, one she could keep, when she was ready to be a mother and a man was ready to be a father, if men are ever ready to be fathers, but now she's forty-five years old and it's too late.

Sarah sighs and goes back inside. She glances around the apartment. There is still so much to do.

Small plants sag on every table, large ones droop on the floor. Sarah has forgotten what their names are. The plants are dying. Good. She can toss them into a green garbage bag without feeling pangs of guilt. As she brushes past, several dry leaves flutter toward the floor.

A bicycle leans against a wall, both tires flat. The apartment is clean though. It looks freshly vacuumed, freshly scrubbed. The sliding glass door to the balcony is invisible; a faint scent of vinegar wafts through the air.

Things have collected here. Pebbles in pottery bowls on the windowsill. Sea shells in tall bottles. A perfect sand dollar; hidden inside it, like a secret, are tiny angel wings.

Whoever moves in here can keep these shells and pebbles or toss them out.

Beside the door, waiting for the movers to take them off for storage, a stack of cartons, most of them labelled BOOKS. Inside one of them there is a field guide with illustrations of all these shells.

Tonight a guy from the used-furniture shop will come by to pick up the bookcases and bed and chairs.

The phone rings. A machine answers: 'No one can take your call right now. Please leave a message after the beep.'

Another voice: 'Hey, Sarah. It's Loreen. Where the fuck are you? Green Talons is on the warpath. A rush job came in that's going to take till tomorrow night. Tomorrow! That's Saturday! She's counting on you, and so am I. I've got a heavy weekend planned. It starts this afternoon, promptly at 4:30. You'd better get in here, pal. I can't keep this guy waiting. He's not the kind who'll hang around.'

Sarah smiles. It surprises her. She thought she'd forgotten how.

She begins to clean out the fridge. But there's so much good stuff: leftover this, leftover that. What a shame to waste it. Sinful, almost.

LEFTOVERS

Sarah plunks down a cardboard carton between the skinny old woman and the young punk one: a half-full carton of grapefruit juice, soda water, a squeezer of lime. Spoons. Bowls covered in plastic wrap: salmon, tomatoes, dill pickles, two hard-boiled eggs. Half a package of digestive cookies. A carrot muffin. A hunk of cheese. A brown banana. Half a loaf of wheat-germ bread.

'Here,' she says. 'Eat up.'

She expects them to be startled, but they're not.

'Great. I'm starving,' says the young woman.

'Digestives. Lovely. They're my favourites,' says the old one.

'I'm going away,' Sarah explains, 'and clearing out the kitchen,' but they're too busy eating to pay attention. Sarah waits for them to thank her but apparently it's not going to happen. She stares at a sailboat heading toward the Western Gap, then walks away.

Nancy and Fern eat until all the food is gone. 'Just in time,' Nancy says. 'I was starving. Who was the woman who brought all this stuff?'

Fern shrugs.

'I thought you knew her,' Nancy says.

They look around. Sarah is once again behind them on a bench, hiding behind mirror sunglasses, maybe watching them, maybe not.

Nancy hollers, 'Thanks.'

'It's okay. I was going to throw it out.'

Seagulls hover and cry, hoping for bread crumbs.

Nancy complains, 'I wish they'd go away. Birds always seem so weird and creepy, like aliens from some other world. I saw seagulls swooping around the sky during the last full moon. They were absolutely silent. It was like a warning. I rushed straight home.'

'I saw pigeons like that once.' Sarah speaks from the park bench as though Nancy had been talking to her. 'Hundreds of them, at dusk. They kept wheeling around and round above the roof of an old picnic shelter on Centre Island. They were silent too. I kept thinking of that Hitchcock movie.'

'Was the moon full?' Nancy asks.

'I've no idea. It was a summer evening. People stood around staring, uneasy, muttering to each other, wondering whether the birds sensed some disaster coming, an earthquake or hurricane or something. They watched a while and then hurried away toward the ferry. Probably they wanted to get home and make love quick, before it was too late. Nothing terrible happened though, and next day everything seemed normal.'

'Do you work?' Nancy asks.

'Of course.'

'So how come you aren't at work right now?'

'None of your goddamned business.' Sarah scoops up the dishes and stomps off.

MISSING STEEPLES, UNMATCHED SOCKS

Nancy pulls a book out of her knapsack, tries to read it, and then gives up. 'I've got to read Anna Jameson,' she says. 'She's on a reading list for school. I want to get the reading over with this summer while I've got some extra time.'

'Who?'

'Haven't you heard of her? She's supposed to be important. She came here in the early 1800s. She hated Toronto and wrote down all her impressions.'

'Complaining's easy,' Fern says. 'Did she do anything about it? That's a lot harder.'

'Well, she wrote about them. Is that enough? Anyway, listen. Here's what she said:

> A little ill-built town on low land, at the bottom of a frozen bay, with one very ugly church, without tower or steeple; some government offices, built of staring red brick; in the most tasteless, vulgar style imaginable...I did not expect much; but for this I was not prepared.

Fern is laughing, doubled over, sputtering as she tries to catch her breath. 'The poor soul. Stuck in these poor vulgar benighted boondocks near a church without a steeple. I'm amazed she was able to stand it. What happened next? Did she adjust? Did her life improve?'

'I don't know. I just got started. I was reading from the first page.'

Fern is choking now. 'Page one, is it? And how many pages of this rant do you have to read? If she's so unhappy she should do something about it. Maybe go from door to door collecting funds to build a steeple.'

'This book isn't supposed to be funny,' Nancy says. 'I think she was unhappy in her marriage.'

'Oh,' says Fern. 'That's different. That explains it.'

She is silent so long that Nancy forgets all about her, is thinking of wildflower names for a baby girl. Violet. Sunflower. Clover.

Fern struggles, trying to hoist herself up from the steps. 'My bones are too old for this,' she says. 'I'm afraid you'll have to help me. I got mad earlier and threw my cane in the water. It was a mistake. Not my first. Probably not the last.'

Nancy hauls her up, and they stumble toward a bench. 'That cold cement. I wasn't thinking. How long have you been here?'

'I don't know. Since early this morning, six o'clock, maybe. I didn't bring my watch.'

Nancy hands Fern her socks. 'Hey! They don't match. I think that's cool.'

'It was dark. I didn't notice.'

'I thought it was on purpose. So why didn't you turn on a light?'

'Someone sleeps in the spare room. I didn't want to wake her up or she'd have insisted on coming along. I needed to be alone.'

'You're not though,' Nancy says. 'What about me? Am I in the way?'

'No, of course not. You don't matter. I've never seen you before, will never run into you again.'

'Do you want to call and tell her you're all right? I think there's a phone booth by the ferry dock.'

'I probably should. I'll be slow though, without my cane.'

'That's okay. You can lean on me instead.'

'Slow down. Don't rush me.'

They cut through the playground. 'I love this place,' says Nancy. 'Look at that happy lion face on the slide. Someday when I have a kid I'll bring it down here to play.'

'When's it due?'

'You can tell? How? I'm only three months.'

'You're keeping it?'

'Yeah, of course. Brad didn't want me to, said I had to choose between him and the kid. I told him, "No contest. I pick my kid." What do you think, Fern? Am I going to regret it?'

'Sometimes. It'll be tough, but you'll be tougher. Anyway, Brad can manage without you. The child can't.'

'My folks kicked me out. They think I can't do it, raise a kid on my own. They say I've got only two choices: marry Brad or let someone adopt it. I think when it comes down to the crunch they might let me move back in. Maybe not though. I guess I can do it on my own if I have to, lots of other women do, but it'll be a lot harder. And I want my little kid to have grandparents. Momma and Daddy would have been such good ones.' She hesitates, stares at the lake. 'I think they wish I'd had an abortion and never told them.'

'I suppose the abortion option makes it hard to decide what to do. But it's irrelevant in this case. You've already decided. You'll be a gutsy parent. Your child's lucky to have you.'

'What about you?' Nancy asks. 'Do you have kids? Did you ever consider an abortion?'

'No. I was already married by that time and it never crossed my mind. Anyway, I'd have been too scared. Abortions were illegal then. You had to have the back-alley kind. People told terrible stories about botched ones. Young girls bleeding to death...'

'Is it going to hurt a whole lot to have this baby? I'm scared of pain.'

'Everyone is. I'm not sure childbirth is the worst pain. How would I know though? The twins were tiny. I don't know what it's like to have a full-size baby. They stayed inside incubators for the first couple of weeks, so I had lots of time to rest up before they came home. But children hurt at the beginning, and they hurt later. Sometimes I think it never stops.'

'Twins? You had twins? Wow! Did you know ahead of time, or was it a shock?'

'They didn't have ultrasound in those days. I had no idea.'

'What did you call them?'

'Stupid names. Willie and Winnie. Wilhelmina and Winnifred. Can you imagine? I thought it was cute at the time. They never forgave me for those names and I don't blame them.'

'Are you serious? They hated the names that much?'

'Of course they did, and as time went on I added lots of other sins to the list. Maybe it doesn't matter. Perhaps daughters are supposed to resent their mothers. After all their fathers fell for us first. It works both ways. Mothers resent their cute little daughters too.'

'Really? How come?'

'It's simple. Daughters are young and beautiful. They're the people we used to be. It's envy, pure and simple.'

'Oh no! Raising a kid is going to be a lot harder than I thought.'

Fern is in the phone booth a long time and comes out looking angry. 'My daughters made me hire this fuss-budget companion. It makes it easy for them; they never have to come and visit, which suits me fine too. We don't like each other very much. But the woman's bossy and tries to order me around. She doesn't seem to realize I'm hiring her, that I'm the one in charge. Every once in a while I have to lay down the law. Is there a pop machine around here? Arguing wastes so much energy. I don't have as much to spare as I used to.'

'Why don't you fire her and get someone you like?'

Fern is silent for a moment. 'I never thought of that. I suppose I could.'

They sit at the ferry dock drinking orange pop, watching taxi-cabs come and go. Travellers arrive and depart, carrying briefcases, looking important. They see the woman who gave them leftovers; she sits on another bench and watches everything. Nancy smiles at her but she ignores them.

A man and child walk past. The man is saying, 'At night the sun moves down to meet the horizon, and the horizon moves up to meet the sky...'

'How about that guy?' Nancy says. 'I can't decide whether that's beautiful or stupid.'

'Ridiculous. And that child has no idea what a horizon is.'

'Yeah. Well, it isn't scientific, but it sure sounds pretty. Like poetry.'

GUCCI GUY WITH CHILDHOOD SWEETHEART

Sarah glares at the women. My God, they're everywhere, ubiquitous as dandelions. Hanging around the dock as though they have some reason to be here, as though they're waiting for the airport ferry and intend to board a small jet.

Sarah feels she owns this place too. She likes to sit here watching travellers, making up stories about them.

Like that guy. Pin-stripe suit, a Rolex, Guccis. A fancy high-powered executive, CEO of a multinational corporation with offices in New York, Tokyo, London. A jet-setter, thinks he's so important. Fifth Avenue apartment, London townhouse, chauffeur-driven limo, the works. He just tied the knot for the fifth time. Serial monogamy, they call it, or maybe serial polygamy, whichever. He makes the same deal each time. If they split up the wife gets the kids, he gets the pets. His parents wouldn't let him have any when he was a kid and he's been making up for it ever since. The current wife's allergic to dogs and cats, so he keeps the animals in a fancy Harbourfront condo with a live-in sitter to give them TLC and food and walks. Every Friday lunch hour he flies in on his private jet with a briefcase full of chew toys and catnip. He pats them for twenty minutes, pays the sitter, is back in his New York office by two o'clock.

Or maybe it's his dear old senile mother in the condo with a private nurse. That's sort of sweet. Flying in once a week to pay his dear old mommy a visit.

No. Sarah's already changed her mind. The nurse is taking care of his childhood sweetheart, the only person he ever really loved. The sweet little thing has a degenerative disease with a long name Sarah can't remember, and anyway wouldn't be able to pronounce. Childhood Sweetheart's no longer able to speak, but of course he knows what she's thinking. She wants to thank him, thank him, thank him. He tells her to blink her eyes if she still loves him, so she blinks her eyes. She isn't stupid. He checks the refrigerator to make sure she's getting high-protein egg nog and fresh-squeezed orange juice. If he has time, he sometimes plugs in the blender himself, and purées bananas and kiwis and mangos which he'd had flown in from South America the day before. He swirls in ice cream or sherbet or yogurt. 'Mmmm!' He licks his lips, rolls his eyes, as though she's a little child, 'Just try a smidgen of this. It's really good!'

The eye-blinking and the blender are multi-purpose, fitting either the dear old mother or the childhood sweetheart version. Probably not the dogs and cats.

PHINEAS BARNUM; THE NORWEGIAN AIR FORCE AGAIN

'I'd like to see what that little airport's like.' Fern says. 'It'd be nice to ride over on the ferry.'

'Okay, let's do it. Come on. What are you waiting for?'

'I think you need to be taking a flight.'

Nancy inquires and comes back to report. 'We're all set. Anyone can go. It costs $2.50 for the round trip and we pay on the way back. Crazy, eh? We get there free but if we don't have money we can't get back. It's like that story about P. T. Barnum's circus, how people followed that sign, TO THE EGRESS, thinking it must be some animal they'd never heard of, then had to pay again to get back inside.'

'His name was Phineas,' Fern says. 'You've got to make allowances for someone with a name like that. It'd be an awful cross to bear.'

'How would you know? Fern's a beautiful name.'

'Ah, you believed me. But maybe I'm really Hepzibah or Petronella.'

The ferry returns and they walk aboard, slowly, Fern leaning most of her weight on Nancy's arm.

'No rush,' Nancy tells her. 'Anyway this ferry ride's going to be awfully short. It's hardly any distance at all.'

'I'm glad they never finished that tunnel.'

'A tunnel? To the island? When was that?'

'Years ago,' Fern says. 'In the thirties. Just before the war. By the time the work got underway the government had been defeated. The Liberals got in and cancelled the whole thing.'

'Good thing,' Nancy says. 'My kid's going to love this ferry ride.'

At the airport Fern looks around and beams. 'This is lovely. It's so peaceful over here. It seems so far away from the city. Picnic tables. Flower boxes at the windows...'

'Yeah. It's great. It doesn't feel like an airport at all.'

They look around the old terminal first. 'This waiting room is neat,' Nancy says. 'It's like a train station. All these nice curved benches.'

'Empty though.'

'Yeah. Sad, isn't it?'

Fern reads a plaque aloud, slowly, as though memorizing it:

... WORLD WAR II... ROYAL NORWEGIAN AIR FORCE TRAINED ITS AIR AND GROUND CREWS... KNOWN AS "LITTLE NORWAY"... 500 OFFICERS AND MEN... SEVEN-TEEN BUILDINGS...

She begins crying. 'It was such a terrible time. I knew some of them. Boys in training to be killed.'

'What happened to the ones you knew?' Nancy asks. 'Did they survive?'

'Most of them. And they kept in touch for a while, sent postcards, that kind of thing.'

'Were you in love one of them? Is that why you're crying?'

'No. It's not that simple.' After a while she continues. 'One day a boy was talking about his girlfriend, how much he loved her. He didn't even know whether she was all right. Norway had already been invaded. That's why they were training over here...'

'Right.'

'I'll never forget how he looked when he talked about her. I realized I'd never loved anyone like that. I was already married to Walter by then and had a sudden glimpse of what I'd missed.'

'What did you do?'

'Nothing.'

'Really?'

'Of course. I was already pregnant with the twins. But even if I hadn't been, it wouldn't have mattered. I wouldn't have considered breaking up my marriage.'

'That's crazy.'

'Maybe, but that's the way it was then. My mother had an expression: you make your bed and then have to lie in it. Meaning, you can't turn back. Carry on. Make the best of things.'

'I still think that's crazy.'

'For a while I thought so too. I'm not sure any longer. The longer I live the less sure I am. Of that, or anything.'

From the restaurant window in the new terminal they watch planes take off and other planes land. A man stands behind a small plane and fumbles with something on the ground. Fern and Nancy stare at him, trying to figure out what he's doing. He walks backward away from the plane, stretching a string of letters on the ground. 'Oh look,' Nancy says. 'When that plane takes off a message will be trailing behind it. Let's wait and see what it says.'

'This is wonderful,' Fern says. 'I always thought it must be nice to be a stewardess. Well I really wanted to fly a plane, but being a stewardess seemed like the next best thing.'

'It's not the same kind of job at all.'

'You're right. This is 1995. The world has changed. Except for me. I've still never been up in a plane.'

'What happened to you and your husband? After the twins were born, I mean. Did you start to love him?'

'Not exactly. I mean, I loved him like I loved my brothers. You know what I mean?'

'I guess.'

'It wasn't fair to him. He was a decent man. He deserved more.'

'Probably you both did.'

'There was a double standard then. Maybe there still is. Men could fool around on the side. They had to be discreet about it so their wives could pretend they didn't know. Maybe some of them really didn't.'

'You knew?'

'I was pretty sure.'

'Is that the whole story?'

'No, of course not. Real life isn't like a fairy tale. It's more complex.' She is silent for a while, then says, 'This is a good time to be having a baby, Nancy. I used to wander through old graveyards and notice how many infants never had a chance to grow up. Back in the old days, before immunization, babies that caught diphtheria or whooping cough usually died. There weren't even antibiotics until after the war. People had so many children because they didn't expect all of them to survive.'

'Also no birth control pill.'

'Oh yes. That too, of course.'

'You visit cemeteries? That seems so weird.'

'I don't do it now. I don't drive any more. But I liked the old ones. Those thin limestone headstones, half toppled over. The flowery verses. Acid rain has corroded them so badly that you can hardly read the words any more, but you can still make out the illustrations, the willow trees or clasped hands or open bible. All that lovely symbolism. Those graveyards seemed so peaceful, maybe because they've been around so long. When I visited them I could almost believe that life made sense.'

As they board the ferry to return to the mainland Nancy picks up a flyer: COME TO FLY DAY. 'Look at this! They're going to have an open house next month. For twenty bucks each we could take a plane ride. You've never had one. It's high time.'

Fern suddenly smiles. 'But would they bring us back? Maybe it's like the ferry. Twenty dollars to take you up. Hundreds more if you want to get back down to the ground.'

'It's on a Sunday. Do you want to go? You'd get to ride on this cute little ferry again.'

'Next month? I don't think so. I'm too old. I don't make plans that far ahead.'

'Well, you don't have to decide right now. There are some more plaques at the other end of the park. I'll show you.'

Fern touches the figures of a pilot and a mechanic sculpted on the side of a stone. She looks at the printing on top. 'I can't be bothered to read all this.'

But Nancy is reading another plaque aloud, 'THIS FLAGPOLE-BASE IS THE ONLY OBJECT REMAINING FROM LITTLE NORWAY CAMP.'

'Except for old folks like me,' Fern says. 'Discarded, or else already dead.'

'You're sure you weren't in love with one of them?'

'No. Not a bit. But their lives seemed exciting. They'd seen so much and I'd seen nothing.'

'Do you want me to read the other plaques?'

'Not really. I'm too tired.' She sags down on a park bench, and closes her eyes. Then a moment later opens them and says, 'Chapman.'

'What?'

'Chapman. The architect who designed those buildings, and the Princes' Gate at the exhibition. You know, the one with an angel on top...' She dozes off for a while, then wakes up crying, 'Oh no! I've got to go the bathroom! Right now!'

Sarah is on her balcony again, muttering under her breath, 'There they are again, that old woman and the punky kid. What's the matter with them? It looks like something's wrong.'

NO PHONE JACK, NO HEART PILLS

Fern is shaking and crying, Nancy frantically looking around. 'I don't see a bathroom anywhere. Can you make it back to the ferry dock? Maybe there's one there.'

The leftovers woman appears beside them. 'What's going on here? What's the matter?'

'Fern needs to get to a bathroom. Do you know where we can find one?'

Sarah looks around. Is there one at the ferry dock? She can't remember. Anyway the old woman probably can't make it that far. 'I've no idea. You'll have to come over to my place. That building right across the street. Come on. Get a move on. I've got things to do. Hurry up, dammit.'

As she opens the apartment door Martin's voice flares, angry, impatient. 'Sarah? Sweetheart? C'mon Sarah, I know you're there. Pick up your phone. You know I hate talking to a machine.'

'Bastard!' Sarah yanks out the phone jack. 'Now you hear him, now you don't.'

'The bathroom,' Fern reminds her.

'Right. First things first. Down the hall. Watch out for boxes.'

'I like this place,' Nancy says. 'You've got so much space.'

'Well, I've been clearing out a lot of stuff. I'm going away.'

'Where?'

'I haven't decided. Whichever way the wind blows. Which is that? East or west?'

'That's so neat. To go wherever you want. You could shut your eyes and stick a pin into a map. Is it scary?'

'Sure. Everything's scary, but staying put seems worse.'

Fern walks toward them, clutching at the hallway wall for support. 'Guess what?' Nancy tells her. 'This woman is going on a trip and doesn't know where.'

'That's right. You can help me decide.'

'I know where I'd go,' Fern says. 'I'd follow the butterflies. Somewhere in Mexico there's a valley that's full of monarchs all winter long. I don't know where exactly, but I'd find out. There are places in California too, but Mexico is where our butterflies go.'

'I went to Mexico once,' Sarah says. 'Acapulco, though. Hotels, swimming pools, happy hours, junky tourist souvenirs. I wish I'd known about the monarchs.'

Suddenly Fern gasps, collapses into an armchair, scrunches her eyes shut.

Nancy panics. 'Fern! What's the matter? Are you all right?' She turns to Sarah and hollers, 'Look at her face! It's grey! Do something!'

But then Fern relaxes again and speaks. 'It's all right. I have weak spells like this once in a while. After I rest for a minute they go away. This one was a bit worse though. Probably because I didn't bother to take my heart pills this morning.'

'Do you have them with you? You could take them now.'

'I'm getting so tired these days, fed up with prolonging things. I think I'm ready to leave. I'm like Nancy though, afraid of pain. But today has been beautiful. I almost missed it.'

'The lake?' Sarah asks. 'Were you...?'

'That was my intention. But I've delayed too long. Now I want to wait around to see Nancy's baby.'

Nancy is holding Fern's hand and crying, but Fern is looking at Sarah. 'Don't put things off the way I have. Go see butterflies, or your own equivalent. Do whatever feels important to you. What's that Latin phrase? A word like a fish. Carp something.'

'Carpe diem. Seize the moment.'

'That's it.'

It's true. She can do anything. Talking to Fern, forty-five doesn't seem old any more. 'I could send you snapshots of the monarchs.'

'That would help.'

RUBY AND THE PASTELS

Sarah donates the cab fare. Nancy climbs into back seat with Fern because they don't think she should be alone.

At the last minute Sarah scribbles her phone number on a scrap of paper, hands it in the car window to Nancy. 'Let me know that she got home all right.'

'Okay, folks. Where to?'

Fern starts to give an address, then changes her mind. 'No. I've moved into a new apartment. Just a minute till I remember where it is.'

'That's okay, Lady. Take your time. I don't want to take you to the wrong spot.'

As they get off the elevator they see Fern's companion standing at the open doorway of the apartment. She strides down the hallway to meet them, already starting to rant. She has been waiting all day to do this. 'What in the world did you think you were up to? Where were you anyway? What a nerve!'

Fern brushes on past her. 'Ruby, for heaven's sake, be quiet.' Once she's inside the apartment she sags onto the couch, awkwardly, too exhausted to move into a comfortable position.

But Ruby can't stop. 'You should never have gone off alone like that! Without even letting me know! You're just lucky I didn't call the police! I guess being arrested would learn you! Your poor daughters were frantic. Imagine scaring them like that! Them having to drive all the way from Waterloo because of this nonsense! They ought to be here any minute.'

'My daughters? You called them? How dare you?'

'Of course I called them! I was frantic. I had to ask them what to do. You were missing. Running off in the middle of the night. You had no right to do such a stupid thing.'

'But you knew I was all right. I left you a note.'

'What note?'

'I shoved a note under your door.'

Ruby leaves, comes back a minute later. 'Yeah, you're right. There was a note, but I never saw it.'

'That's not my fault,' says Fern.

Ruby spits back, 'Not mine neither.'

'Oh, for heaven's sake be quiet,' Fern says. 'I've had enough. Get your things packed. I want you out of here tonight.' But she's interrupted by a banging on the door, voices, the sound of a key turning in the lock. Two middle-aged women rush through the door, hollering, 'Ruby, what's happening? Have you heard anything?'

Then they see Fern flopped on the couch, and both shout, 'Mother! You're back! Are you all right?' Then they notice Nancy. One asks in a frosty voice, 'And you are...?'

Nancy stares. They are clones, except for the different shades of their clothes. It's hard to believe they're related to Fern. Club women, is the word she thinks of, a word from some novel she didn't like. Fashionable matrons with painted nails and perfect make-up. Designer clothes in pastel colours, expensive, understated. Nancy wonders whether they discussed their clothing ahead of time. 'Let's wear our sweater and skirt sets, our matching sandals, the triple strands of pearls.' Were their faces already made up, or did they stop to apply eye-liner, lip-liner, blusher, before dashing out the door?

'And you are...?' Pink Twin asks again.

'Nancy. A friend of Fern's.'

Ruby interrupts. 'Your mother tried to fire me. Imagine! What a nerve.'

Fern raises herself up on one elbow and speaks emphatically, 'I certainly did. Why aren't you in the bedroom right now packing your clothes? Hurry up.'

'Mother.' Pink Twin speaks slowly, distinctly, too loud. 'You can't fire Ruby. You need to have someone with you. You can't stay here all alone. We'll put you into a nursing home if we have to.'

Mauve Twin interjects, 'That's right, Mother. You can't fire her. You're just not capable of making a decision like that.'

Nancy is getting fed up with these bossy daughters. 'Of course Fern's capable,' she says. 'If you want someone to stay with her then you'd better find someone she likes.'

'I'm not staying where I'm not wanted. That stupid old biddy. She never does what I tell her. I'm out of here. The sooner the better. Write out my cheque while I'm getting packed.' Ruby stomps off, ignoring Pink Twin who's chasing after, pleading, 'No, Ruby. Don't go. Don't bother packing. Mother needs you. We'll get this sorted out.'

Mauve Twin stays in the living room trying to calm Fern down. 'Okay now, Mother, just settle down. Try to relax. You need to have someone with you. You know that. If you don't like Ruby we'll find somebody else, but she'll have to stay on until we find a replacement.'

'No.'

'You'll just have to put up with her for a few more days whether you want to or not. A week, at the most.'

'No. I want her out of this apartment right now. Nancy will stay with me until you find someone else.'

They both look at Nancy. Mauve Twin asks, 'Can you do that? Stay with Mother for a couple of days. Would you mind?'

A roof over her head. No more all-night bus rides. She won't have to beg her parents to let her come home. She can let them stew a little, wonder where in the world she is, whether or not she's all right. 'Sure. I can do that. It'll be fine.'

After Fern drops off to sleep the pink woman boils water for tea. Mauve Twin sets out cups and saucers, spoons, while Pink Twin fetches the sugar bowl, pours milk into a pitcher. Nancy watches as they move around each other in the cramped kitchen, never colliding, as though they've been practising all their lives, And they have been, she realizes, manoeuvres probably learned while still in the womb. They write down their phone numbers in Waterloo, tell her to call if there are problems. They take turns talking. 'Here's the cell phone we got for Ruby. You don't have to be with her every minute, but when you go out we want Mother to be able to reach you.' With hardly a pause the other takes over, 'Call her every hour if you're going to be away very long.'

'Why do you boss Fern around like that?' Nancy asks. 'Talking down to her like she's a little kid. She's a grown woman. She should decide things for herself.'

But they assure her they have the right. Fern signed a power-of-attorney paper when she was so sick the doctors expected her to die.

'But she's okay now,' Nancy says. 'Why don't you rip up that piece of paper? Let her live the way she wants to.'

'She's not capable any more. Mother's changed. She was independent before she took sick, and she was beautiful, aristocratic, her silver hair always shining. All that sparkle left her. It was the illness that did it, and the hospital stay. She went in young but came out old.'

'But at least she came out,' the other says. 'And now we have to make decisions for her, decide what's best...'

'And how she spends her money,' Mauve Twin adds. 'We have the right. She can't stop us.'

'I'll...' but Nancy stops herself from saying, 'I'll ask my daddy. He studied some law. If he doesn't know he can ask one of his friends. They're all lawyers.' Anyway, her daddy won't talk to her right now, maybe never again. 'I need to go to bed,' she says instead. 'I'm exhausted. It's been a big day.'

'Listen,' Mauve says. 'You don't understand. This is our mother. She's our responsibility. We have to look out for her, make sure she's safe.'

'What about happy?' Nancy asks.

'Happy, sure. But her safety comes first.'

Nancy has to think about that. Which one is more important? But it's too late right now. She's exhausted and fakes a yawn. It works; the pastel twins leave.

Finally she remembers to phone the taxi-fare woman but the phone rings on and on. Probably the phone jack is still out of the wall.

FIRST DAY

Next morning over coffee Fern and Nancy stare at each other in amazement. 'I can't believe how quickly everything happened,' Nancy says. Fern doesn't answer, just looks confused. She must remember what happened, Nancy thinks. Of course. How could she not?

'Fern...' she begins. 'You do remember firing Ruby yesterday? That I'm going to stay until the twins find someone to replace her?'

'I don't know...'

'You don't remember your daughters being here? Don't remember meeting me at Bathurst Quay?'

'Oh, for heaven's sake, don't be foolish. Of course I know that. I just can't think of your name.'

Nancy laughs in relief. She prints her name on a scrap of paper, tapes it to the refrigerator. 'If you forget again, just sneak a glance at the fridge.'

Nancy looks around the apartment, tries to understand this new place she's moved into. She opens the kitchen cupboards, one after another, tries to figure out where things are kept. On the counter is a glass of water containing Fern's dentures. Beside it pill bottles are lined up according to the size of the tablets inside.

It takes a while for a routine to be worked out.

It turns out Fern doesn't eat breakfast, so Nancy tries to skip it too, but finally breaks down, discovers bread, can't find a toaster. Fern doesn't exactly eat lunch either. She's a grazer, grabs a few crackers every time she's near the kitchen, then eats them as she wanders, leaving a crumb trail behind like Hansel and Gretel. She'd have no trouble finding her way back.

That afternoon the phone rings, one of the twins, 'How is Mother?'

'She's lying down. Is there a message?'

'It's her daughter Winnifred. Is everything going well? I realize Mother isn't easy to get along with.'

'We're fine.'

'Well then, I'm wondering how long you can stay.'

'I'm okay here. I'm not in any hurry to move out.'

'But how long? A few days? Weeks? Months?'

'Sure. A few months would be fine.'

'Aah.' A sigh of relief. 'Good.'

'Hold the phone a second. I hear Fern getting up. You can speak to her yourself.'

Click.

At supper time, that first night, they each wait for the other to start cooking something. Nancy's afraid of intruding; Fern just doesn't want to be bothered.

Finally, 'We could take turns?' Nancy suggests.

'You start.'

So Nancy rummages through the fridge, finds some eggs and scrambles them. Next night she waits and waits for Fern to start cooking, but it doesn't happen. 'I'll cook again tonight,' Nancy says. 'I might as well do it while I have the time. When I start school it'll be different.'

But it won't be. Fern doesn't cook. Anyway, why should she? She isn't hungry, couldn't care less whether she eats or not. She has eaten food day in, day out, year after year, all of her life. Enough's enough.

LABELS

Now that Ruby's gone Fern can relax. She knows Nancy's on her side, and won't phone the twins to make reports. Fern can say whatever she wants, is free to yatter on and on about nothing. She can sort through jigsaw puzzle pieces of her life, and make up stories about her past, creating versions she can live with. Nancy won't know whether they're true or not, won't even care.

'Look at all these books,' Fern says. 'Presents. Every Christmas and birthday, year after year. As if people thought I'd read them. No way. Why would I fritter away my time reading novels, books about people who don't even exist. Anyway I had my own life then, had things to do. I was busy all the time. I never bothered to read these stupid stories then, am certainly not going to waste what time is left looking at them now. Out they go. Garbage stories. Want them?'

If Nancy says yes she has to take them now, right this minute, and store them with her own things. If she says no Fern tosses them toward a carton in the corner. Later she'll label it either SALVATION ARMY or GOODWILL, whichever charity she likes better on the day the carton's full to the top.

Fern has lost so much weight lately. She tries on old flowery dresses, one after another. They droop around her ankles, limp and shapeless, as though they're still draped on hangers in her closet. She shoves the dresses in green garbage bags, then hands Nancy a package of stickers, an old present from one of the twins. 'Probably supposed to be a joke,' Fern says. 'They certainly knew how much I hated cooking.' So Nancy takes another cutesy stickum label with pink flowers around the edge. Beneath intricate 'FROM THE KITCHEN OF' letters she prints, WOMEN'S SHELTER: CLOTHES, in black marker.

Now that Fern's so skinny her dentures don't fit well either. She only wears them when she eats, then drops them back inside a glass of water until the next meal, whenever that is. As if food matters to her these days, as if it tastes good like it used to. Nancy can cook whatever she wants, so long as she remembers to buy the ingredients ahead of time. Luckily the twins keep a stash of money in a jar inside the kitchen cupboard.

Fern sometimes eats, sometimes can't be bothered. She feeds on memories instead, sorting, deciding which ones she wants to keep, wondering how to get rid of the rest.

GOLDFISH

Nancy is rested, feeling good. She leaves Fern's place, finds a bus stop, heads downtown. She has things she ought to do: talk to a school counsellor about skipping the second semester, inquire about day care, drop in uninvited to see how the staff treat little kids, especially babies.

At least she doesn't have to worry about tuition. She's lucky about that. Her grandma left education money when she died, earmarked, so it couldn't be spent on anything else.

Nancy doesn't get off at the subway though, just keeps on going, exploring the city, putting off her errands, afraid of them somehow. Talking to the counsellor will make the baby in her belly seem real. The thought of staring at little kids in day care scares her even more.

Maybe tomorrow. Why not be carefree for one more day? Pretend not to be a person at all.

Maybe a goldfish, a fantail, the graceful feathery fish she has seen in the ponds at parks. She is beautiful, the same colour as blazing sun. The sun shines at her and she shines back, both of them dazzling, reflecting each other. Other people don't even notice how she shimmers, as beautiful as gasoline rainbow spills on the street. Nancy hides behind the tinted window of the bus and wants to warn strangers to be careful: don't look at me unless you're wearing sunglasses, don't take a chance of burning your eyeballs, don't look, don't dare look. She has a pocket thesaurus in her backpack and searches for colours that could describe her: gold of course, but also umber, pumpkin, melon, cantaloupe, henna...

A crying baby distracts her and she slams the thesaurus shut. When she has a child of her own she won't be able to play games of pretending. It's the kind of silly thing a kid might do. She'll have to take giant steps and act like a grown-up.

But not now, not this soon. She's still in her teens. Just barely though. Nineteen. She'd better enjoy being a teenager while she still can. Not for much longer. Just one more month.

That crying baby is driving her crazy. Nancy wants to yell at it to shut up, wants to complain to the bus driver for allowing such a racket, but settles for glaring at the mother instead. Doesn't she know how to keep her own baby quiet? Then a sudden realization: oh no! Pretty soon people will stare at her and think the same thing. No! NO NO NO! She's not ready to grow up yet. No way she can let this happen, a bunch of baby cells surging inside, multiplying like a mathematical progression, growing bigger and bigger, taking over, distending her belly, stretching it out of shape. No way she wants another person inside her, bumping around, elbowing her organs, making her awkward, off-balance, ugly. No way she'll ever be able to finally shove a huge baby out her bottom.

No way she wants a baby anyway, having to take on all that enormous responsibility, teach everything it needs to know. She's too young, hasn't learned enough yet, isn't ready. She should have had an abortion while there was still time.

Too late now. She's going to be a mother anyway. A single mother. That boring cliché. Always irritable, exhausted, having to do everything all by herself. What in the world has she been thinking of?

Nancy panics, pulls the signal cord, jumps off the bus and starts running. Anywhere. After a couple of blocks she stops and looks around. Where in the world is she? She checks her pockets, finds change for a pay phone.

Fern answers the phone, finally gets tired of waiting and shouts, 'Speak up. Don't bother deep breathing at me, Mister,' and hangs up.

Nancy dials again, her voice a faint whisper, 'I'm scared.'

'Well, of course. Why wouldn't you be? Get right back here so we can talk about it. Come on home as fast as you can.'

Home. Nancy thinks about that as she retraces her footsteps, finds the right bus stop, and heads back.

When she arrives, the kitchen looks festive. Fern's fancy company teacups are on the table, and yellowing paper serviettes left over from some long-ago birthday. A rosebud plate holds stale cookies Fern has found somewhere. She pours cold water into the teapot though. Nancy can't decide whether to tell her or not, doesn't want to embarrass her, and finally settles on letting Fern find out for herself when she tries to pour the tea and drink it. But Fern doesn't want any, doesn't even bother to pour it for Nancy, is too busy talking. When Nancy finally puts water on to boil, Fern doesn't pay attention.

'No one ever feels ready. You're just the same as everyone else. All women feel scared, but they don't know it's okay to admit it. I was terrified and probably your mother was too. Suddenly you get a glimmer of what you're getting into. Nobody really thinks it through in advance. No woman who gave it enough thought ahead of time would ever get pregnant, ever dare have a child, take on that total responsibility for someone else's life. They'd never risk having sex.'

'The race would die out.'

'Maybe that's why we don't think it through. Survival of the ones who act instinctively, who have sex and get pregnant and carry the baby to term, who are more scared of having an abortion right away than of giving birth later on. At least now we know what caus-

es it. In ancient times people didn't even know there was a connection between intercourse and pregnancy.'

'You're kidding.'

'No, of course not. Why would they make the connection?
Morning sickness doesn't start right after conception, as soon as the
couple climbs out of bed, and it takes almost a year before the baby
arrives. I don't know how those ancients ever figured it out. It must
have taken them a long time. A lot of generations.'

'That didn't stop them though, once they realized, once they
made that connection, cause and effect.'

'It still doesn't. Parenting doesn't have to make any rational sense.
It's an act of faith. Faith that you can do it, that you'll stay healthy and
alive for another couple of decades, that folks will help you when you
need it. The responsibility never stops. For twenty years I didn't dare
relax or look away, afraid something terrible might happen.'

'Twenty years! That's way too long. I'm not ready to give up
that much of my life for some little kid I've never even met.'

'What would you rather do instead?'

'I'm not sure. I always wanted to do something creative. I don't
know what. I can't paint. Maybe acting, maybe writing. Something
people will remember about me when I'm gone.'

'What about growing a baby inside your belly? Surely that's
about as creative as you can get.'

'Anyone can do that.'

'That's not true. Men can't. Maybe that's why there are more
male artists than female ones. Women don't need a paintbrush or a
pen to express their creative urge.'

'It's not the same.'

'No. Of course not.'

'I never wanted a baby. I'm afraid I won't love it.'

'You will. Don't worry about that. Women always love their
babies. It's instinctive. Maternal instinct must be some kind of hor-
mone, secreted like breast milk.' Fern changes the subject, hoping

Nancy doesn't ask when hers disappeared, whether it was ever there in the first place. 'What about coffee? I think there's a jar of instant somewhere.'

'None for me. Maybe I'll drink herbal tea from now on. Caffeine's not good for the baby.'

Fern hugs her, awkwardly, as though she hasn't had much practice. 'Good for you.'

Later Fern asks, 'What about adoption? Have you given it any thought?'

'Are you kidding? This is MY kid. MY responsibility. How could I be sure someone else would raise it right? But you have to promise me you'll hang around. This little tadpole-child's going to need a grandma.'

'Maybe your parents will change their minds. Probably they just need a little time to get used to the idea.'

'Maybe, maybe not. Another six months is all they've got. Anyway, they kicked me out, Fern. How could parents do something like that? I'd never do that to MY kid. I'll always be there for it no matter what.'

Fern doesn't answer.

TOYOTA AND CEMETERY

'Do you know how to drive?' Fern asks. 'I have a car somewhere. I was supposed to sell it when my eyes got bad.'

'Where is it?'

'The twins probably think I really did.'

'Where's the car, Fern?'

'I forget. Out in the suburbs somewhere. In clone country. Somebody I knew had a double garage. Half of it was just sitting there empty...'

Nancy reads names aloud from Fern's address book until Fern finally remembers.

The car is waiting, a Toyota hatchback, 1984, but with hardly any rust, probably because Fern only drove it in nice weather. 'Where do you want to go?' Nancy asks.

'Just keep driving. Maybe we'll come to a cemetery. It has to be old though. I'm not interested in new ones.'

'A cemetery? Are you sure?'

'They're so peaceful, and a nice reminder that life goes on. Our ancestors have been here. They've had their turn and now they're feeding the earth that supports our feet. There's a cycle of life, a pattern. Nothing wasted. I think that's beautiful, a comfort.'

Behind a stone fence beside a church at Pape and O'Connor they find some old gravestones, but the wrought-iron gates are padlocked shut.

There is a plaque. Nancy skims it, reads sections aloud. '*The Taylor Cemetery… the Primitive Methodist Connexion in 1851… a brick church in 1859… The family operated… paper mills… a brick mill in the Don Valley…*' but Fern's already too tired to listen. 'That's enough,' she says. 'I want to go home.'

She goes straight to bed, while Nancy makes arrangements to store the car in the parking garage under the apartment building. Later Nancy looks up cemeteries in the phone book, places to take Fern before school starts. Later on they can visit on weekends. It's a weird way to pass the time, but if that's what Fern wants that's what she'll get. Nancy owes her.

CEMETERY CONCERT

Nancy packs a picnic lunch. 'C'mon,' she tells Fern. 'The sky is blue. It's a cemetery day.' She has read in the newspaper about noon-hour concerts at a cemetery in North York.

The place is so peaceful. Fern closes her eyes and lets the music surround her, and the scent of flowers. Occasionally she opens her eyes and glances around. A bronze seagull. A reflecting pond. Beneath a mirror of the cloudless sky, in a tangle of water lilies, orange shadows dart back and forth. Near a sundial with hiero-glyphic symbols, the words, *'It's later than you think.'*

Fern recognizes most of the plants in the herb garden. 'And look. A catalpa tree. My favourite. My grandparents had one in their backyard when I was a child. This place is lovely. Thank you. It's been a perfect day.'

'There's a greenhouse too. Do you want to walk through it?'

'No. This has been lovely. I don't want to spoil it by getting tired out. It takes too long to get my strength back.'

Fern waits in the car, dozing, while Nancy wanders among gravestones. She writes down a few inscriptions in her notebook to show Fern later: *'Together again.'* *'To live in hearts we leave behind is not to die.'* An open book: *'May thy hours be long, and thy days be bright, may thy cares be few, and thy burdens light.'* She reads the plaque beside the office: *'William Lyon Mackenzie is said to have hidden on the prop-erty... following the rebellion of 1837.'*

She wants to remember this place. Some day she will bring her child here and they will talk about that grand old man.

Next day they return so Fern can visit the greenhouse. She studies each plant, says the names aloud, 'Crown of Thorns. Queen of the Night.' As they leave, Fern turns back and stares, perhaps memorizing, perhaps saying goodbye.

LETTERS FROM SARAH

A bulging envelope arrives, stuck in the mail slot. 'You open it,' Fern says. 'It's too big. I can't be bothered.'

'Okay. Oh. They're a bunch of letters from Sarah.'

'Sarah?'

'Don't you remember? The woman who lived at Bathurst Quay. Who was packing up and moving away.'

'I'm too tired to look at all these papers. You can read them.'

'Out loud?'

'If you have to.'

Dear Fern,

Are you okay? That girl with blue hair was supposed to phone and let me know.

Dear Fern,

Hope this reaches you. I tried to remember the address you gave that taxi driver. Hope I've got it right.

I'm almost on my way.

I'm in a line-up at the bus terminal, waiting to buy a ticket on the next bus. I'm leaving right away for somewhere, wherever they've got.

There's a skylight in this building. Blue and mauve rectangles alternate. Magritte clouds float inside a Mondrian sky. I never noticed this before, never took the time to.

So long Toronto. Hello somewhere else.

Dear Fern,

The next bus was headed for London, the passengers already boarding, so I bought a ticket, thoughtless, casual, like all the decisions I've made or not made in my life, and climbed up the steps as easily as if it was any local bus taking me to work or home again. It headed west for a couple of hours, then unloaded in London. Not very far from Toronto, but it's a start.

I'm staying in a seedy furnished apartment. The builder economized on the walls, and probably everything else. In the next room two strangers are fucking against the night. Outside the window a jogger's feet are pounding the pavement to the same beat. And me, I'm just staring at the patterns of cracks along the walls. Also writing this letter.

Dear Fern,

No monarchs yet. No milkweed in this pristine right-wing city.

Be patient. I'll head south soon.

Dear Fern,

How are you? Are you all right?

Ignore these letters. Toss them straight into the recycling box unread. I don't want to burden you with my grumbling. You don't deserve it, and have enough problems of your own.

I'm on a rant these days. I never knew there was so much anger inside me. Maybe if I write it down in letters and throw them away inside a mailbox the anger won't find its way back.

Poisons. Toxins. Tears like acid rain. Maybe they'll drip on this writing paper, cause it to disintegrate.

Dear Fern,

I spend my time in libraries acquiring useless information. Anything for distraction. This time I'm reading about whales.

The grey whale migrates too. Like monarch butterflies. Like I intend to. It bears its young on the breeding fields off the Baja peninsula, then travels 9,000 kilometers to feed in the arctic seas. 9,000 kilometers! Imagine! Orbiting back and forth inside its cold environment, rhythmic, persistent, as constant as the frozen moon. Do you think it knows what it is doing? Does it think that it has a choice?

Probably not. Too close to have perspective, to see its pattern as we see it, maybe it's far enough away from me to figure out mine.

'Isn't that beautiful?' Nancy says. 'Too bad you can't write her back. She forgot to include an address.'

'Good.' Fern mutters. 'I don't want to anyway.'

MOVIE

Nancy phones up some girlfriends from high school, makes plans to meet them at a donut shop, go to a movie. She tries on one T-shirt after another, because she doesn't want them to suspect she's pregnant, doesn't want Brad to find out.

They're so boring. Nothing has changed inside their lives. They talk only about boys, have no interest in anything else: which one is cute, which one looks as if he might ask her out, should she phone him if he doesn't...

Nancy wants to shake them, tell them to pay attention, listen to what they're saying, give it more thought. What if the boy does ask the girl out, what if they decide they like each other enough to fall into bed. Nancy wants to holler at them, 'You could get pregnant! Think about it! Pregnant!'

'Hey, Nancy. You're awfully quiet. What's happening? What's new?'

'Nothing much.'

It's all she can do to keep her mouth shut. 'One time he forgets to bring a condom, but you're both too carried away to care, to make a rational decision. After all, how could just one time matter? So you have sex anyway, you don't decide to, you just do it. A missing condom. It only has to happen once but it changes everything in your life!'

The movie is supposed to be funny. Her friends are giggling, laughing. Nancy is laughing too, hiccuping, crying aloud, and laughing louder to cover it up. Her friends look at her and then laugh louder. Are they laughing at her or the movie? She isn't sure. She wants to shake them, to shout, 'Pay attention! I'm pretending life is funny, but it's not. Look at me! Believe me, these are real tears!'

STILL LIFE W. AMARYLLIS PLANT

When Nancy gets home Fern has been crying. 'Tell me something, anything,' Fern says. 'Distract me. I've been thinking about my daughters and that always makes me sad.'

So Nancy tells Fern the amaryllis story. 'This is a true story,' she says. 'It really happened.

'But every time I say the word, with, don't picture the written out word. You've got to imagine I'm only using a 'w' plus a period after it. That's the way our home-room teacher, Mr. Willis, always wrote it on the blackboard: w. He did it all the time, not just for math and science, for everything. I still think it's cool, like shorthand, a secret code.

'My life pretty much came to a standstill last Christmas, w. nothing but an amaryllis plant in my life. And at first it was only a bulb.

'It came w. a page of instructions: "Keep in a warm place." Well, good luck. Whoever wrote that had no idea how cold our rec room could get. All the furnace vents headed upwards. I lived underground then, like a mole maybe, or an ant inside an ant farm. Tiny windows up near the ceiling, w. bushes in front to block out the sun. Dark and gloomy, lovely, like living inside a cave. I pretended I was living in some ancient age, a cave-woman, prehistoric. Life must have been hard in those days, but probably the rules were simple. But mostly I just pretended I was grown up and had already moved out, was renting a basement apartment in some stranger's house. Ignoring my family, and them ignoring me right back. Going in and out the side door, just as though it was a separate apartment. I could go upstairs whenever I wanted though, and at first I went up there a lot, for eating or watching TV, but then less and less often. No one ever came downstairs. They promised me that. Mum would leave the laundry basket by the basement doorway and put a note under the door so I'd know it was there. I washed and dried and folded their laundry, all the towels and bedding and clothes. A pretty small price to pay for my privacy. My friends were jealous. They couldn't believe my folks would leave me alone.

'So I'd explain, "That way we don't fight. We all like it better."

'I had lots of privacy, especially w. Brad. And we needed it, our hormones bubbling inside us like ginger ale.

'That's really why they did it. Because they didn't want to know we were sleeping together. They didn't want to admit it. My dad especially. He wanted to believe I was still his sweet innocent little girl.

'I could have put the amaryllis bulb beside the furnace, probably that would have speeded it up, but I wanted to watch. What if something happened and I missed it? Brad bought it for me as a Christmas present, a 2-for-1 special, the other went to his grandma, for her nursing-home window.

'I told him, "I'll bet she likes it. It's a great old-lady gift." Meaning not great for a girlfriend. He finally figured it out and we had a fight. So I had lots of time to watch that plant grow because we broke up on Christmas night. The plant's fault, right?

'How come he gave it to me anyway? He was so stupid. He must have known I wanted something personal. Some kind of jewellery. A charm for my bracelet. A ring. A pendant w. my name engraved on the back.

'A huge bulb wrapped up in plastic, not small and neat like an onion, but textured, rough. Like a huge scrotum is what I thought, but never said. Except hard, woody, like the swollen bumps on old gnarled trees.

'I planted the bulb in a potting soil, watered it once a week. And started watching. I watched it a lot. Brad was gone and I had nothing else to do. I watched and nothing happened.

'A whole month went by like that. Nothing to see but the very top of the bulb, the potting soil, the plastic pot w. a matching plastic saucer underneath. Nothing changed, but I kept staring anyway, studying, paying attention, afraid something would happen and I'd miss it. It might as well have been a painting, those crayon shadings of brown, lighter and darker. Still life all right.

'I asked everyone, "How come some plants come from bulbs instead of seeds?" Not even my teacher knew, but he looked up amaryllis in his big dictionary, and said it's the Greek word for country girl. I guess long ago in the fields of ancient Greece there lived a girl named Amaryllis. I'd stare at the bulb w. nothing happening and try to imagine what her life was like.

'I watered it once a week from the bottom. The bottom! Imagine! As if it could matter. What if it was growing outside, in a field or forest? I tried to picture some bottom-watering place, maybe an underground spring like Banff that smells of sulphur. Okay, but also no top-watering at all, some place where rain couldn't find it. That's a lot harder. I tried and tried to imagine some place like that, but a greenhouse was all I could think of. No place in nature. Failure again. No wonder nothing was happening. No wonder I was left w. nothing but an amaryllis plant in my life.

'I got flower books from the library. Guess where it grows? South Africa. This plant was as close to gold and diamond mines as I'll ever get. Guess what else is in the same family? Onions and garlic and chives and leeks! Also daffodils and narcissus. And something else called snowdrops, whatever they are. I hope they're as pretty as their name.

'Finally, when I was ready to throw it out, a green nubbin appeared. Eventually it turned into leaves and a stem.

'I'd see Brad at school. We'd pass in the hall and sometimes speak. "Hiya." That's all. Sometimes he'd be w. his new girlfriend. I didn't know her. She was only in grade ten. Chewing gum w. her mouth open, laughing too loud, her skirt shorter than everyone else's. That kind of a girl. I wanted to tell him, "Try giving her an amaryllis bulb for Valentine's Day. See how much she laughs at that."

'He'd wait for her every day in all the same places he had waited for me. Like, didn't he have any imagination at all? Couldn't he think up new trysting spots? I learned that word tryst in English.

From Shakespeare. I really like it and try to use it a lot. Even though it always looks misspelled, like a vowel is missing.

'They'd hold hands in hallways and neck in corners. I pretended I didn't notice.

'Are you okay, Fern? Are you bored? This is a real story. It's awfully long, but I don't want to leave anything out. It's a story that grows slowly, like that amaryllis plant.

'The spiky leaves decided to grow sideways instead of straight up. The thick stem went in the opposite direction. Maybe it is supposed to happen that way for balance, but if so it didn't work. The plant kept falling over. I tied the stem and leaves together so it would look right, but then the thing toppled over again. I tried leaning it into a corner, propping it against a table, but nothing worked. It kept tumbling over. I wondered how often a plant could try suicide before being successful. Apparently quite a lot.

'I kept rescuing it too soon, while it was still alive. Like my friend Suzy. Did I ever tell you about her? Sneaking tranquillizers from her mother's bedside table but then getting impatient, swallowing too quick, before she had saved up enough. She warned us all never to do it because stomach pumping is really gross.

'Pets and pet-owners gradually resemble each other. I read that somewhere, and got wondering, maybe plants and plant-owners ditto. I wanted the plant to grow up to be beautiful, symmetrical, graceful, just in case. I kept thinking, someone should study this. But not me. I didn't have time. I was too busy watching that gawky amaryllis plant.

'Maybe in nature an amaryllis grows inside a jungle where other plants help hold it up.

'That girlfriend was always fastened to Brad, clutching at his sleeve, twining her finger through his belt loop, as if that would keep him from getting away.

'I still remember interesting facts from those flower books. In Japan people pickle cherry blossom petals, and then cook them into soup. Can you imagine? Yuck! And apparently violets stand for faith-fulness. Why couldn't he have given me a violet instead?

'The plant kept toppling over, no matter what I did. I tied it too loosely, afraid of damaging it. It was getting top-heavy. There were three ugly lumps at the top of the stem. White, but a little bit pinkish. Like snake heads. Eyeless albino ones, blind. I was scared to get too close in case a snake head darted forward, w. a forked tongue flicking out. Zap, zap. Instantly I'd be dead.

'I've seen that Cleopatra movie and shut my eyes when she got bitten. Dying that way must be scary. Anyway a snake bite probably hurts. I decided that if I was ever serious about suicide I'd try some other way. Not pills like Suzy, but a bridge or subway train or razor blade.

'I tied the plant to a table leg w. a heavy piece of rope. It seemed like bondage. I kept apologizing to it a lot.

'I read aloud to it from the library book, telling interesting facts. Moonflowers open only at night. The biggest flower in the world is in Indonesia and weighs fifteen pounds. The leaves on a compass plant turn toward the sun and then go back to normal at night.

'The snake heads on the plant were growing, getting longer and fatter. They still seemed ugly.

'Something woke me up in the middle of the night. I lay there scared, wondering, Could a plant do that? Did it make a noise? Maybe. Because something was happening to it. Slowly. Very, very. In science class we used to watch films of flowers opening, but speed-ed up, time-lapse photography. I wanted to speed up my amaryllis plant like that.

'It took so long.

'Maybe some day I'll work in a flower shop. I think I'd like that. Where old people w. creaky bones buy pots of tulips and hyacinths and daffodils. They buy them in winter, forcing the plants to flower early, in case they don't make it all the way through to spring. The old folks, I mean, not the plants. College boys buy corsages of sweetheart roses for college girls to pin on pretty party dresses. A bride orders flowers for her special day bouquet. A groom buys a white carnation to wear in his buttonhole. Celebrating all those happy times.

'Or maybe I could work in a greenhouse like at that cemetery in North York. The air smelling fresh and damp and sweet. Soft light drifting through misty windows onto green leaves all around me. Plants growing, using up carbon dioxide, making fresh oxygen for people to breathe.

'The biggest snake head opened slowly, like the mouth of some blind creature just emerging from beneath the earth, or arriving from another planet in a scary science fiction movie. The amaryllis mouth opened up, ominous, like that.

'I peered inside w. a flashlight. Nothing to see. The petals curved inward, so carefully, trying to hide the colour inside. Almost hiding it, but not quite. I can't describe the colour: pinkish cream, green-tinged, that's the best I can do. It was brand-new, pure and virginal, untouched.

'Probably all new flowers seem innocent and sweet like that, even the flesh-eaters, those Venus fly-traps.

'The plant was taking all night to open. I kept worrying that I'd fall asleep next day at school.

'The flower opened up so wide that the petals changed direction and started curving outward instead of in. Six of them, beautiful, creamy, w. a fine line of pink at the very edge, like it had been drawn w. a pink pen, the edges torn in a few places, as though the change from curving forward to backward had been too sudden, violent, traumatic. "You don't know anything about it," I told that amaryllis. "Be glad you aren't a human baby, and don't have to overlap your head bones to squeeze through a birth canal. Be glad you're not a human woman either, your tender private place being stretched apart." I remember thinking I'd never let a baby's head bones get a chance to squeeze out of me. Huh! What did I know?

'If this amaryllis was looking for sympathy it had come to the wrong rec room.

'The flowers tipped downward. I had to lie on the floor to look inside.

'Long tendrils were exposed now, a pistil, six stamens w. little nubbins of pollen fastened at the ends. Adrift in the rec room air, reaching out, hopeful. Too bad. No bumblebees or hummingbirds in this basement. No butterflies either. Forget about pollination, plant. All that sex stuff only causes trouble anyway.

'Next day after school I saw Brad waiting for me. He said he missed me, wanted me back. I asked, "What about the little sex-pot in mini skirts?" He said, "Oh her. She's all right, but it's all show. She's just a C.T.," and then watched to see if I knew what he meant.

'I told him off. "How dare you call her a cock-teaser? Geezus, Brad, she's just a kid. She shouldn't have sex unless she wants to. Not until she feels ready." He tried to put his arm around my shoulder, but I shoved him off, told him to get lost.

'Then I headed for home, almost skipping, like a little kid in grade school playing at recess. It was a lot more fun saying no to Brad than having him say no to me.

'The flowers started to droop. Maybe they needed more sun. "Sorry plant," I told it. "What you see, this rec room, this still life, is what you get. Look around. Enjoy. It's not so bad."

'But of course that's not really the end of the story. Brad can be such a sweet-talker when he wants to. So remorseful. Eventually we did get back together, just long enough to get a baby started.'

Fern is silent.

Nancy glances over, realizes she's asleep.

September

DECISIONS, DECISIONS

It's September, already September, and Nancy begins to panic. She's supposed to start her community-college course in less than a week. 'Should I start? Should I even bother?' She keeps asking Fern this over and over. 'Is there any point taking the first semester when I'll probably never be able to finish the course? Should I try to earn some money instead?'

'Don't ask me,' Fern says. 'I don't know. I really don't. It's your life. Yours and the baby's. You have to decide for yourself. You're all grown-up now and get to make your own mistakes. I don't want you blaming me later.'

She says, 'I don't know,' meaning I don't care. As if I've ever known what's right, as if I've made wise choices in my *own* life. As if it matters to me what anyone else does. Even Nancy.

Nancy keeps asking until Fern finally gets fed up. 'Stop nagging at me about it. Ask someone who can give you some useful information. Someone who's graduated from the course, maybe, or a student in her last year, or a counsellor at the school.'

'Yeah. Right. Okay.' Nancy knows she should have thought of this herself. It's good advice. All the same she tosses a coin: school or not. It comes up heads, meaning yes.

'Okay, I've made a decision,' she tells Fern. 'I'm going to school. Anyway, I might as well. They already have the cheque for the first semester. It's probably a hassle to get it back.'

A hassle, Fern thinks. As if this decision-making hasn't been. 'Good. That's that,' and she closes her eyes, pretends to sleep. She feels exhausted. Nancy takes too much of her energy. These days she hasn't any to spare.

'Wake up,' Nancy is shaking her shoulder. 'C'mon. All that school decision stuff was hard work. We need a break. I've heard of a neat cemetery downtown. An old one. Let's go and browse around.'

An old cemetery. Good. Fern is already in the car before remembering she wanted a nap.

ST. MICHAEL'S CEMETERY

Nancy drives north up Yonge Street past St. Clair, then makes a U-turn and drives back down again. 'This is the right intersection. Okay, where is it?'

She parks the car and they walk along Yonge Street, past stores, one after another, nothing but stores. No green space, no gravestones.

'I'm too tired for this,' Fern mutters, but Nancy isn't paying attention. Just ahead of her a woman is pushing a baby carriage, and Nancy speeds up so she can peek inside. 'What a cute baby,' she says. 'How old is she?'

'It's a boy.'

'Oh. Sorry.' Then she remembers Fern and looks back.

Fern has stopped. She is leaning against a variety store, holding her hand out. 'Give me the car keys. I need to sit down. I'm too old for all this wandering around.'

'Okay. I'll keep looking.'

Finally, from the parking lot behind an office building, Nancy sees tombstones behind a chain-link fence. Nancy goes back and gets the car, drives Fern along side streets looking for an entrance. Usually they can't get a glimpse of the cemetery at all. 'Are you okay, Fern? Can you just wait here in the car while I walk up Yonge Street again?' This time Nancy finds it. 'There's a dead-end lane between two stores,' she says. 'Isn't that great? A natural pun. Have you rested up enough, or would you rather come back some other time?'

'When you get to my age,' Fern says, 'you never put things off.'

The gate is open, but a couple of big guys with German shepherds are sauntering among the gravestones. They're pretty intimidating-looking, so Fern and Nancy pretend to study the *Trespassers Will Be Prosecuted* sign. They read the rules and regulations, learn a tiny section in the south-west corner contains people who died outside the pale of the church.

'Pale?' Nancy asks.

'A boundary. Like a palisade, a fence around a fortress so the defenders are safe inside. Believers, in this case. Dead ones. Safe from the dead infidels buried outside.'

'I think that's crazy.'

'Well, it's religion. It doesn't have to make sense.'

Finally the guys leave and Fern and Nancy go inside. A few birds sing, a bee buzzes somewhere nearby, but otherwise the place is silent. They are surrounded by old statues and crosses, tomb-stones.

Nancy points to a small building shaped like an octagon. 'What in the world is that?' and goes over to check it out. 'Hey, Fern. Listen to all this: *The Catholic cemetery is a holy place... blessed by the church... a place for worship, prayer, and reflection upon divine truth and the purpose of life... the resting place until the day of resurrection for the bodies of faith-ful departed... temples of the holy spirit... souls are now with God...*'

'Enough, enough,' Fern protests. 'I'm ready to go home.'

FLY DAY

On Fly Day the airport is crowded. Banners are fluttering. Children crowd around someone who swelters inside an animal suit. 'I liked it better without all this clutter and confusion,' Fern complains.

'You know what I read in a magazine once?' Nancy says. 'To try looking past it. Looking through and beyond. You could try. It sounds stupid, but maybe it really works.'

The pilot of the little Piper Cherokee looks worried when he sees Fern. 'You'll need to walk across the wing to get inside. Can you manage?'

'Fern is gutsy,' Nancy assures him.

'I'll bet you're the oldest passenger I've ever had,' he tells Fern. 'How old are you anyway?'

'I forget.' She points to Nancy, 'This woman is probably carrying your youngest.'

'Just sit back and enjoy the ride,' he says. 'Relax. It won't hurt a bit.'

'Are you sure?' Nancy and Fern clutch hands, just in case. But the pilot isn't paying attention. He adjusts switches, talks to the control tower, taxis into position. 'Ready?' he asks.

And they are. A blue sky is waiting to be explored.

Stupid drips of salt betray her. Fern meant to be fiercer, never permit them, but take-off, that irreversible act, unnerves her. She wants to unfasten her seatbelt, scream at the pilot to return.

Beside her Nancy chatters, 'Look at this, Fern,' and, 'Hey, look at that!'

Fern brushes her off like tears.

MORE LETTERS FROM SARAH

Dear Fern,

So how are you? Are you feeling okay?

Here I am in London. The wrong one. It rains here though, just like in the right one.

Another rainy day today, and I was almost hit by a grey Honda while jaywalking across Richmond Street to get a takeout coffee and carrot muffin. I was feeling blissful, listening to my Walkman, humming along while Jennifer Warne sang Leonard Cohen's First We Take Manhattan. Skidding a little, because the tread's worn off my sandals and they slide out from under me on wet pavement, and squinting upward looking for a rainbow because the sun had just come out. The sun slanting into my eyes and onto the windshield of a rusty '81 Honda where a woman was fiddling with the volume dial on her radio, the Cowboy Junkies suddenly hollering, I'm So Lonesome I Could Cry, so loud I could hear it over my Walkman, while she was trying to soothe or else drown out a crying baby in the backseat that kept on screaming, screaming, screaming anyway. I jumped aside, fast, without thinking about it, and the Honda missed me. But it was so close. All that metal, rigid and ungiving. I suddenly realized how fragile my soft skin is, how much terrible damage a car could cause.

It's a Monday. Well, of course.

Me weeping tears of relief that the car hadn't hit me. Mouthing prayers of thanks to the traffic gods or someone. Heading off to a cinema to celebrate survival. Buying a jumbo-size bucket of popcorn. They asked if I wanted salt. No thanks. I can cry my own.

Dear Fern,

I've signed on at a temp agency, which means meeting new people in new offices all the time. But the good thing is I get to leave them and move on. I don't want to get to know them. I think I'm turning into a nomad, a recluse.

People are so phony. They pretend to be into sincerity these days, even almost strangers like the folks I run into at work. Their eye contact lasts too long. They say, 'Tell me about yourself,' and expect me to be able to answer in one sentence, an edited version prepared ahead of time. They want truth, but just a quick one, abbreviated, a sanitized précis. I haven't figured out a truth that short.

I don't like people any more. Sometimes I wish the human race would die out so the world could become a better place. Humans were a mistake. Surely an all-knowing god would have figured that out by now. Why doesn't he sit down at his creation computer and reformat, or else delete, delete, delete.

Of course, individuals are a different matter. I like most of them, have even loved the odd one. But humans in general, as a collective, NO. Enough's enough. Erase.

The neutron bomb was almost a good idea, except it would wipe out all the other creatures too, the innocent bystanders: earthworms, great blue herons, pandas, dust mites, elephants, right whales, plankton... Plankton? Is that animal or vegetable? I'm not sure. Maybe the bomb wouldn't wipe out plankton.

We need one that's more specific, wiping out only human beings, leaving the other animals unharmed. Yo scientists. Practise on. Don't give up yet.

Dear Fern,

Someone is singing on and on, forever singing in the next apartment. Someone strums fingers against guitar strings and sings to those gentle chords. Nothing is happening in the world except this music, this accumulation of sound. The earlier notes don't go away; new ones keep being added to them. I seem to be drowning inside this music, notes splashing over and over, pulling at the edges of my mind, the way an ocean pulls at a shoreline until the sand disappears inside it. Tuning forks thrum inside my ear drums, vibrating against my mind. The music keeps on and on, it never stops. A voice, a guitar, a keyboard, speaking in some pre-language I don't understand. A message I need to remember and hold on to. There is so little to hold on to any more. Only this music that never stops, that goes on and on.

TIME TO GROW UP

'It's time to grow up now,' someone is saying in Nancy's dream, a woman's voice she can't recognize. Not Gramma's, not Momma's. Maybe her own.

All her life people have been asking this difficult question, 'What do you want to be when you grow up?' Momma and Daddy finally stopped when she got hostile, but everyone else continued on: relatives cornered her at family gatherings, neighbours stopped her on the street, teachers pestered her at school. Nancy never had an answer ready, but got tired of being polite. She wanted to holler, 'I won't be a busybody, anyway. I'll be someone who minds her own business, and leaves other folks alone.' She keeps on going to school, year after year, surrounded by students who chatter about their career plans, who seem to know who they will turn into. She attends all the way to the end of high school because she can't think of anything else to do.

Her friend Amanda quit at the end of grade eleven and now she's a receptionist in a big law office downtown. She answers the phone briskly, 'BryceLiptonMortonBestandFish,' whenever Nancy calls. She says this with confidence, as though it's all one word and has meaning. 'All law offices have long names,' says Amanda, who has learned important facts like this about the world.

'But what do you do all day?' Nancy asks her. 'Just answer the phone politely and put people on hold? Sit customers down in a waiting area where they can read magazines and fall asleep?'

'Clients. Not customers. We call them clients.'

'Don't you get bored? Don't you go crazy?'

'Nope,' Amanda explains, 'I just put in my time. Okay, so it isn't exciting, it's not rocket science exactly, but what do I care. Every Friday they give me a cheque.'

Nancy can imagine answering the phone, glancing at letterhead on the desk so she'd be able to parrot the company name correctly. But then what? Then what? The person at the other end would say something, maybe ask a question, and Nancy would have to know how to reply. How did Amanda ever learn this?

'Time to grow up now,' the dream voice keeps saying, until Nancy wakes up and realizes it's true: it IS time for her to grow up and learn how to be a mother.

'Let's go visit another graveyard,' she calls to Fern, putting it off.

FAKE FLOWERS

Mount Pleasant Cemetery is huge, impossible to miss it, but easy to get lost inside. By a fountain behind the office a wedding party is posing for photographs.

Nancy and Fern drive on to a secluded spot, pour peppermint tea from a thermos, and listen, at first to silence, and then, as their ears become attuned, to one bird call after another. Different songs. What kind of birds could they be? Then the sound of a jogger's footsteps, lub dub, like a pulse beat, long before he's in sight. 'I like this place,' Fern says. 'Things are happening here. Life goes on.'

A car parks beside them, an elderly man unloads a push mower from the trunk, cuts the grass over a grave. He replaces the mower and gets out clippers, trims longer grass around the stone, then pokes artificial flowers into the earth. 'The staff maintains the grounds,' he tells them, 'but I like to give this one an extra trim anyway. My wife. She always liked things kept neat.'

While Nancy wanders from one labelled tree to another Fern lies down on a bench to rest, flat on her back, eyes staring upward. 'Go ahead,' she tells the sun. 'Blind me. See if I care.' She can dare to be reckless; it's a dull day so she knows she's safe.

Above her, leafy branches have captured jigsaw puzzle pieces of the sky. A sudden breeze, and she watches the branches toss this way and that, knocking puzzle pieces in all directions.

The sweet scent of mown grass floods her nostrils until she wants to cry.

Fern wants to yank off her shoes and socks and wander around, earth mother, barefoot, the fresh-mown grass staining her feet. She thinks there's some taboo about walking on graves, disturbing the dead. That's the only thing that stops her.

JOLLY JUMPER

'Hey Fern! Look! Someone in the next building was throwing this out so I grabbed it. It's supposed to hang in a doorway so a little kid can jiggle up and down, while it watches its momma cooking sup-per or washing dishes. Isn't it great? Did you have one of these for your kids?'

Fern didn't, and at first can't remember why.

That night Fern has a nightmare. A hook is fastened to the top of a door frame. She is a little child, looking up at it, maybe five or six years old.

She wakes up and remembers the hook. It is fastened in the kitchen doorway. Mommy hangs a cheesecloth bag of crabapple mush that drips into a pail. As soon as there's enough Mommy will cook the juice to make jelly, then pour it into jars with melted para-ffin wax on top. 'Watch out,' says Mommy. 'Be careful.' It's hard to get in and out of the kitchen without bumping into the pail. Did she knock it over once when she was a toddler? She can't quite remember, but all the same Fern lingers in the dark hall, afraid to enter the kitchen. Are flies buzzing around or not? Is there a louder humming, perhaps a bee? Does a trail of ants snake across the linoleum floor, or is that some other time? Fern is a big girl now, in kindergarten or grade one already, but all the same she lingers at the kitchen doorway, afraid to go inside.

Sometimes her baby brother's jolly jumper hangs from that hook.

Fern's brother and a neighbour's long-haired baby sit in a playpen in the middle of the living-room floor. Her brother pulls the other baby's hair. He always does this. At first the other baby ignores it, but finally it begins to wail. The neighbour puts down her teacup with a sigh. She unfastens Fern's brother's hands. She hands the babies hard teething biscuits to chew on. As soon as the neighbour sits down again Fern's brother grabs the other baby's biscuit. After a while he pulls its hair again. Neighbour tells her long-haired baby, 'Pull HIS hair. Do it back.' Fern's mother gets huffy about this, but anyway it doesn't matter. The neighbour's baby won't do it, is probably scared to. Fern wants to pull everyone's hair, her mother and little brother, the neighbour woman. Except for the poor little long-haired baby whose hair has been pulled too much already.

Fern thinks she can remember spinning that jolly jumper around and around, her little brother laughing at first, then screaming as he crashes into the door frame, bumping his head. Her mother rushing in to see what's wrong, then screaming too. 'Get to your room. Right now, young lady.' Chasing Fern up the stairs, swatting her bum with a fly-swatter at every step. 'You'll be sorry. Get in your room and don't come out. Just wait till your father gets home. He'll give you what for. Just you wait.'

The neighbour with the baby moved away and was replaced by Mrs. Jenks who has tables cluttered with china knick-knacks Fern can look at but mustn't touch. Fern holds her hands behind her back, afraid she might forget. Uncle Bert's house is on the next street. In the backyard he has a matching dog house for his Irish setters who wait patiently all year for him to take them hunting in the fall. The Davidsons' car has a rumble seat they can open up in back. Sometimes they offer Fern a ride to school, but she always refuses politely, afraid it might snap shut and trap her inside. The MacDonald kids at the corner have a train track set up in their basement all winter long. They keep adding more and more buildings made out of matchboxes: houses and stores, churches and schools; they rip off pieces of an old sponge, painting them green to look like trees and shrubs. They're allowed to have paint and brushes and toy soldiers and Meccano. They can invite all the neighbourhood kids in to play. Their parents don't mind. Fern stares at those parents when she sees them on the street. They look so ordinary but they're not. They let their kids play at anything; they don't care about noise and mess.

Years later Fern would go back to that old neighbourhood and wander one street after another, trying to relive her childhood, hoping to improve it, talking to ghosts.

FINALLY SCHOOL BEGINS

Nancy's first day of school. Fern can hardly stand all the confusion. Nancy bolts down breakfast, packs a lunch, fusses with important pieces of paper, can't find her backpack. Finally she is gone, slamming the door behind her, and Fern can begin to relax. At last, she thinks, finally I can have some peace. But within ten minutes she is bored, has no distractions, nothing to do. She can't remember how to pass the time. What in the world did she do before?

Nothing, maybe. Because Fern has no life now. She tries to remember when she had one. She rereads yellowed newspaper clippings:

> Ferns will decorate your home and brighten your life. Open a window, let a breeze into your house, and watch the leafy fronds waft to and fro, creating intricate patterns of light and shadow on the ceiling and the walls.

Fern riffles through photo albums, tries to climb inside old snapshots. She daydreams of those long-ago times, tries to believe she was ever a sweet little pinafore toddler, school-girl with braids, teenager in cardigan and pleated tartan skirt. What did she dream of in those days? How did she imagine her life would go? Not this way, that's for sure. Dwindling down to nothing, growing old, getting forgetful, more and more ugly.

Today Fern pretends she's middle-aged, a stodgy snapshot matron who paces one street after another trying to pretend nothing has changed since she was a teenager, thirty years ago. Thirty years. People hide inside these houses who could remember her if they tried. Middle-aged Fern could ring their doorbells and ask whether any pieces of truth can be found in her old family stories.

But she does not want to meet them and make conversation. 'Hasn't it changed?' they would ask, meaning the neighbourhood, and she would say, 'Yes,' meaning herself.

But even that's not true. Surely this self is who she's always been: middle-aged mother of teenaged twins, her hair and skin greying, her curves softening, sagging. Unloved. Maybe her husband never even loved her in the first place. This rejected self is the only one she can be sure of.

She hears old stories of herself as a child or teenager at family gatherings, even repeats some of those stories herself, but no longer believes them.

Or does she?

Fern's parents buy a car. When she comes out of school at the end of the day she finds them parked out front, waiting for her to look over and notice them and be surprised. On the car radio a man is talking; he keeps interrupting their conversation. Her parents don't pay attention to what he says, but Fern tries to listen to everybody at once and gets confused. Poppa and Mommy keep smiling. Poppa drives up and down every neighbourhood street, slowly, so people will notice. 'Well, what do you think?' he asks, so Fern knows she is supposed to think something but has no idea what. 'Oh my,' she says. It seems to be enough.

One day Fern and her mother stand at the front window and watch a stranger drive the car away. 'What's he doing, Mommy? Where's he going with our car?' Fern asks. Her mother is crying. 'The bank. The bank's taking it.' Fern knows her mother's lying. A person is doing the driving, and anyway a car can't fit inside the doors of a building.

Is that when they move to a small apartment? The halls are dark and scary. One day a tenant suddenly grabs Fern, shoves her against the wall and pushes his bumpy body against her. It feels awkward and uncomfortable, ridiculous. He kisses her hard, his moustache bristling against her face. He is skinny but very strong. Fern hardly knows him, just to say hello when they pass in the hall. She doesn't want to talk to him, much less kiss him, but of course knows enough not to be rude. Her mother has taught her to mind her manners, always be polite to grown-ups. The man has an English accent and Fern assumes the accent has something to do with it, that all English men must be like this. An apartment door opens along the hall and he suddenly lets go, tells Fern to go away, hurry up about it. At the time she doesn't make the connection, doesn't realize he's afraid of getting caught. She is as innocent as a baby. Keeps wondering why he quickly shoved her away, what she had done wrong. Wasn't she polite enough? Did he realize she did-n't like it?

Did she ever tell her mother? Probably not. What words would she have used? Anyway, adults are allowed to do what they want; Fern is still a child and has to do whatever she's told.

The sound of a key turning in a lock. A young woman bursts through the door. A stranger. What in the world is she doing here?

'Hi, Fern. Did you miss me? Let me tell you about my day. I think I'm going to like this school.'

'What, what...?'

'Hey, what are you doing? Looking at snapshots? Can I see?'

'Oh. Nancy. Fine. Yes. You're back already.'

BIRTHDAY

Nancy sits in the school cafeteria. She pretends she isn't moving, that the earth beneath her is fixed in place, inside a universe that remains constant, doesn't contract or expand.

Nancy sits still, the earth tipped on its axis, balancing. She tries to balance too. Precarious.

All the cells in her body are getting ready to betray her. She is twenty today, a teenager no longer. This is the moment her body was created for. Until now it has been preparing. Right now she is at her Everest peak; she is as perfect as she'll ever get. From now on she will move downhill, slowly at first, imperceptibly, feeling her way, then gradually picking up speed and momentum, afraid of stumbling, the world moving past her too fast, before she can truly appreciate it, while she's still trying to understand it, to truly enjoy.

Macroscopic changes in the universe. Microscopic changes inside Nancy.

Twenty. Today is her birthday. Fern doesn't know. Only Nancy's family knows, and she won't phone them. No. She definitely won't.

But finally she gives in. She does call and her mother answers, 'Nancy! Is that you, dear?' Then Daddy's voice, an angry shout, 'Don't talk to that slut.'

The dial tone drones on and on, like an angry bee in her ear.

Nancy storms out of the phone booth, out of the school, and strides along one unknown street after another until she calms down. Eventually she finds her way back to Fern's and enters, bringing take-out chicken as a treat. Rationalizing the expense: it's her birthday, after all. She should do something to celebrate.

'I've brought a chicken box,' Nancy says, but Fern mishears, remembers fussy toddlers, flushed and feverish.

Fern swabbing cool calamine on their chicken-pox spots. Comforting, cuddling, feeding sips of flat ginger ale. Singing nursery rhyme songs over and over until her voice gives out. It seems like chicken pox goes on forever. It seems like childhood does.

She doesn't notice her little girls keep growing older and taller, doesn't realize these moments will disappear forever like fevered rashes. Memories to be safely stored, stoppered inside a pink lotion bottle.

In her own childhood a blue Vicks jar was kept on the window-ledge because every time Fern had a cold it always settled in her chest. Her parents hovering above her bed, cool fingers soothing her forehead, an old frayed handkerchief of her father's covering the sticky ointment on her chest. Fern, cushioned in quilts and semi-darkness, too miserable to realize she was happy.

Were her daughters ever as happy as that? Were they sure of her love? Of Walter's? At least they had each other. Fern hopes that was enough.

'Eat up,' Nancy says. 'I didn't buy this chicken just to look at.'

TIRED

'I'm fed up with feeling so tired all the time. But I'm four months now. Maybe I'm supposed to be this way. Anyway, at least I've never thrown up in the mornings. I guess I'm lucky about that.'

'I remember being exhausted,' Fern says. 'I was tired for years. Until the twins started kindergarden. Maybe even longer.'

'Oh well, twins. Of course. Did you know what to expect?'

'Do you mean the fatigue? No. I think every new mother discovers that for herself. Of course I wasn't expecting twins either. I knew I was enormous and terribly awkward, so I expected a really big baby.'

'Weren't there twins in your family?'

'No. There may have been in Walter's, but he was adopted so we had no way of knowing.'

'Wow! Twins! What a shock!'

'When the first one was born it was so little I could hardly believe it. And then about ten minutes later another one came along. Maybe the doctor suspected ahead of time, but if so he didn't warn me, probably wouldn't have thought it was any of my business. In those days patients knew nothing. We just did what we were told.'

'Like taking whatever medicines were prescribed?' Nancy asks. 'You wouldn't refuse them? Wouldn't question whether there might be some other treatment?'

'No. Of course not. Doctors seemed like gods then. We obeyed them. We thought we had to. We didn't know we had any choice.'

LETTERS FROM SARAH

Dear Fern,

It won't leave me alone. Martin's face seems to hang suspended on the wall before me, then it moves off when I do, floating beside me like Alice's disembodied Cheshire cat. I try to get away, close a door quickly, but it slides easily beneath and looks reproachful. It shines bright on the pillow beside me, and keeps me awake, my eyes weeping from the relentless incandescence of his face.

He was my best friend. I don't know how to talk to anyone else.

Dear Fern,

There's not enough love to go around. It starts in childhood. Our parents can't possibly love us enough. Not as much as we want or need.

Each child needs to be loved best.

We grow up looking for that missing love, and search for it all the rest of our lives. After all, we're entitled, we know we deserve it, so we hang on tight to any little bits that come our way. We're stingy, go through life afraid to part with any, afraid to love first, or love too much, deplete our stock. We don't want to give some out unless we're sure we'll get back just as much, or maybe even a little bit extra.

That's what's wrong with the world. Ask anyone who's ever been a kid. We all know we were short-changed but don't realize everyone else was too. How come no one talks about it? How come we didn't compare notes with other kids, discover we weren't alone?

But we couldn't tell. It was such a shameful secret, not to be loveable enough.

Mothers lie. They say everything will turn out all right. Of course they lie. They're supposed to. It's their job. Sometimes they let a piece of truth slip out by mistake, but it's okay: whenever that happens we don't believe them.

Dear Fern,

I should have been a sculpture in a gallery, a stone woman by Henry Moore, surrounded by warning signs, 'HANDS OFF. DON'T TOUCH. DON'T TOUCH.'

Dear Fern,

Did I ever tell you how Martin and I got started? Well no, of course not.

I was going crazy with some problem or other and needed to confide in someone, so picked a nice married guy at work, someone I figured I could talk to. An older guy. Maybe I thought that meant he'd be wiser, or maybe I'd already intuited that he liked me. Surprise, surprise: it turned out we got along, had the same zany sense of humour. It was so predictable. We went to bed, felt terrible about it afterward, swore never again, but then... That ancient story.

He cheated on his wife, so of course I knew that sooner or later he'd cheat on me. I kept waiting for it to happen. But for a long time we were happy. Maybe I should be satisfied with that.

I'm trying to remember that blissful couple, those simpler times.

One December, Christmas shopping, our parcels scattered beside us on the ground, outside the entrance of the old Massey Hall on Shuter Street, snowflakes drifting down like petals tossed from white spirea bushes, while we held hands and swung around in circles like little children. It was the most carefree moment of my life, flying through the damp confetti snowflakes and grey city grime.

I wish I believed in other dimensions, could think that sweet innocent couple still exists, that somewhere they're still swinging.

When I watch other couples they don't look sweet and innocent at all.

CEMETERY: ST. JOHN'S NORWAY

'I've heard of a cemetery you might like,' Nancy says. 'In sociology class we were talking about death rituals. Funerals, tombstones, epitaphs, things like that. Sometimes on a child's gravestone there's a lamb or an angel or a dove. They're symbols of innocence. Did you know that? One of my classmates remembered seeing a lamb on a child's gravestone. It was in a cemetery she used to cut through on her way to school. St. John's Norway.'

'Norway?'

'Yeah. I don't know why they call it that.'

'Maybe Norwegians are buried there.'

They drive down on a sunny day. 'Maybe we shouldn't waste our time here,' Nancy says. 'Look! The lake is just down the street. We could skip stones on the water instead.'

'Later,' Fern tells her. 'Let's look at the gravestones first.'

'I like the fancy gate.'

'It's called a lych-gate. The place they used to keep the coffin until the minister arrived.'

'Under that little roof?'

'I guess so. I'm talking in the old OLD days. Before my time.'

The cemetery is deserted and quiet. Sounds seems to come from far away: the mournful sound of the airbrakes on the Woodbine Avenue buses, the screeching of the streetcar wheels along the tracks on Kingston Road.

Nancy finds an obelisk with an urn on top. 'There's a lamb,' she says. 'Maybe that's the gravestone she was talking about.' Children are listed on three sides, and an adult on the fourth.

'Imagine raising a family in those old days, in the eighteen-hundreds. It must have been terrible.' Fern says, 'That poor mother. Her child dead, only three years old.'

Nancy looks shocked.

'But it's not like that now,' Fern reassures her. 'Children survive. They take vitamin drops and thrive.' She leans on her cane and looks around. 'What a nice place,' she says. 'But where are all the Norwegian boys?'

Nancy checks in the cemetery office, and reports back. 'No. This neighbourhood was called Norway in the old days, back in the 1800s. Maybe someone from Scandinavia settled here and thought the scenery reminded him of home.'

At a store on Queen Street they buy ice-cream cones, then drive on down to the lake. Fern dozes in the car while Nancy wanders along the boardwalk. She comes back chanting nursery rhymes. 'I'm going to bring my kid here,' she says. 'This city is full of nice places for my little girl to explore.'

'Or little boy,' Fern reminds her.

'I keep thinking of it as a girl. But it doesn't matter. I'll love it like crazy, whichever it is.'

LITTLE NORWAY AGAIN

While Nancy's off at school Fern rummages through old snap-shots, arranging and rearranging, being selective, finally fastening some in albums, ripping others out, the waste-basket at her feet cluttered with whatever bad memories she wants to discard and forget. Glossy black and white relics, and the negatives that spawned them. At first she searches through heaps of negatives, holding each one up to the light, squinting, discarding this one and that, but finally getting fed up, tossing them all out, every one she finds, good ones as well as bad. Transparent ghosts. Like Hiroshima shadows traced on a sidewalk. 'Out, out, damned spots,' she mutters, for some reason thinking of Lady Macbeth. 'Stop cluttering up my life.'

She tosses out old phone bills, bound in elastics, sorted by year. Old birthday and Mother's Day cards from her daughters, doesn't even reread them. Old love letters are all she'd want to keep, if she'd ever received any.

Long ago there was a war. Fern remembers a chain-link fence down by the lake, a sentry box at the entrance. 'Why didn't I take pictures of Little Norway?' she mumbles. 'Why didn't I keep the letters from all those sweet Norwegian boys?' The thank-you notes for dinner invitations, the scribbled airmail letters from overseas.

Oh, those old days. Fern is lost, awash in memories.

She and Walter are still dabbling at being a married couple, practising, like children playing house. They own fancy plates and cutlery, and a table with a starched white tablecloth to lay them out on. Matching napkins folded neatly. How old is she now anyway? In her mid-twenties, a good ten years younger than Walter, but she feels so old already, as though everything that could ever take place has already happened. She's a married woman already, a matron. She knows sex secrets, things her mother had never told her, never even hinted at.

She'd been a baby bride, still in her teens. Sweet little innocent virgin, with breasts that had never been touched, hymen intact, ready to spatter red blood on the bed sheet.

> Ferns are hardy. All the same, treat them with care. They do best when left alone. If you must transplant, do so only in the spring.

But now she's in her twenties and she and Walter are an old married couple. Fern has learned to cook fancy meals so they can entertain.

Visitors arrive every Sunday for dinner: young Norwegian men who are Fern's age and training to be airmen. 'It's the least we can do,' she and Walter tell each other. Fern needs distractions, because talking to Walter is getting harder and harder. They seem to have nothing in common. At the time she feels so clever, suggesting the visits, thinking she's putting something over on him.

Now, suddenly, at age eighty, years and years later, long after Walter moved out, after his death, she realizes he must have hated their weekends together too, had probably welcomed those visits as much as she had, maybe even believed it was his idea.

One night they're invited back to a party inside the compound. A brightly-lit hall. Music. Young couples dancing, sweet, graceful, vulnerable. Walter refuses to dance, believing it's sinful, but Fern dances all night anyway and Walter won't speak to her afterward. He is silent for a whole week, thinking he's punishing her. As if she cares.

Fern loves dancing. Before Walter, right up to the Saturday before her wedding, she goes dancing every weekend. Live bands play at all the dance halls: the Silver Slipper, Club Top Hat, the Palace Pier, the old Bucket of Blood beyond the boardwalk at the foot of the hundred steps.

She dances as often and as fast as she can. Quick, before she marries a Walter, a Baptist who thinks it's sinful, because she has suddenly realized she'll never be able to go dancing again.

JUNK

Nancy finds snapshots in the garbage when she's cleaning up from supper. 'What are these? Can I look? I love old photos. Oh wow! This baby in an old-fashioned wicker carriage. Is it you, Fern? And this toddler with a sandcastle on a beach? Is this you or one of the twins?'

'Me, me, me. Me as a baby. Me on the beach. Then getting married. Wearing my happy-face mask with Walter and the girls. Junk. All of it.'

'Can I have a couple?'

'Whatever you want. Just keep them out of my sight or I'll throw them out again.'

'Maybe you should save them for your daughters.'

'Those brats! They don't deserve them.'

All the same, after Fern is safely in bed, Nancy gathers up the photos. She keeps a few, hides the rest in a plastic bag. Some day the twins may want them.

MONARCHS

Fern rummages through snapshots, but mostly memories.

All those nice fresh-faced Norwegian boys, learning to fly. Just imagine! Fern used to daydream all the time then, imagining what flying might be like, all alone like a bird or butterfly inside the empty sky. That space, that freedom. She wouldn't recognize any of the men now. Of course not. They wouldn't know her either.

War-time. It affects everything, changes their lives. Walter's so upset about failing his physical, especially because of something invisible, a heart murmur. 'Why couldn't it be a limp?' he complains over and over. 'Then strangers wouldn't stare at me like I'm yellow.' He grumbles about this so often that Fern finally gets fed up. 'Would you rather have a palsy?' she asks. 'Or epileptic fits? An amputation? Wear dark glasses and carry a white cane? Then folks would understand and make allowances. They'd forgive you for not wearing a uniform.'

King and country. Patriotism. The words mean a lot to Walter, whose uncles fought in World War I. All through his childhood he'd played with his lead soldiers and daydreamed of war, of mustard gas, hand-to-hand combat, muddy trenches. Fern can't relate to this at all. Why should she care about all those foreign governments, squabbling, always wanting to grab each other's land. 'Our grandparents came to Canada to get away from all that,' she tells him. 'Those countries are on the other side of an enormous ocean. Why should we care what they do?' Eventually she changes her mind though, as young men from her old neighbourhood begin enlisting. She starts knitting like everyone else: warm socks and balaclavas for sailors in the North Atlantic. Hovers around the radio listening to the rhythm of Churchill's oratory. Sympathizes with stammering King George, the nice new monarch with a beautiful blue-eyed wife who wears pearls around her neck. They have two sweet little princesses who aren't twins but wear matching clothes as if they were.

Monarchs. Butterfly kings. 'Once when I was a butterfly...' Fern thinks, that same old mistake she makes over and over. Has she said it aloud? Anyway what difference does it make? She's all alone. Or is she? She looks around. Nancy must be in her own room, or else outside. Even so Fern wants to get it right, 'Once when I saw butterflies...'

Monarchs. She is a child again, maybe ten years old, lying on the grass beneath a maple tree, a dying one covered in brown leaves. All the rest of the trees in the park are still green. It's a nice park beside the gothic library with heavy wooden cathedral doors. What was it called? Kew Gardens. Yes.

A monarch circles. As it lands on a branch the brown leaves shiver, bits of orange flicker, then disappear. The leaves settle back to drab.

Fern stands up on tip-toe and stares intently: those things looking like dead leaves, can it be? Are they the undersides of butterfly wings?

Fern squeezes her eyes shut and then opens them again, in case she has dreamed it. The butterflies cling to the branches like brown leaves waiting for an autumn breeze. Fern waits. Another monarch lands on a branch, more flickers of orange. How many butterflies? she wonders. Perhaps fifty on a branch. How many branches?

She lies beneath the tree, the drab undersides of butterfly wings dangling above her. She wants to stay here with them fluttering above her forever. Or else shake the branches and watch thousands of butterflies flutter upward together, as though the tree was flying. The sky would be transformed into a church window, sunlight shining through stained-glass wings. Butterflies. Pieces of orange sun.

Monarchs, and on only that one tree in the whole park. Fern knows this, because she checks them all. It is late summer. The wind is strong.

She runs home and calls her parents to come quick and look. They don't believe her. 'A tree full of butterflies?' scoffs Grandma. 'Ridiculous. The child's had too much sun.' Mommy drags her off to bed, kicking and screaming, and next day won't let her outside without a hat.

When she runs back to check, all the butterflies are gone.

Monarchs. Kings of the sky. Fern would like to see a butterfly tree again.

Years later Walter tells her about seeing a town full of butterflies, while he was in California on a business trip and taking a bus tour along the coast. The driver said he'd show them something special, not on the route, probably hoping for big tips.

Fern wonders what those passengers expected. Not butterflies anyway.

'Monarchs everywhere you looked,' Walter tells her. 'Covering cars and lawns and houses. Signs warned not to kill them or else you'd get a fine.'

'That's crazy,' Fern says. 'How could the bus drive through the town? How could cars?'

'Real slow,' he says, 'so the butterflies have time to fly away.'

Fern doesn't believe him, the way her parents hadn't believed her, but years later, after he moved out, she read about the town in *National Geographic* and almost phoned him to apologize. Maybe she did phone, she can't remember, but it's the kind of mistake she might make.

A whole town full of butterflies, wouldn't that be something special to see? You could store the memory in your mind and bring it out whenever you needed to feel blissful.

You could tell it to your children like a bedtime story. Did she ever do that? Did Walter? Probably not...

A key turns in the lock, the door opens. Nancy. Suddenly it's 1995 and Fern is an old woman again.

'How was your day?' they ask each other, smiling, making polite conversation.

DONEY

Nancy sees a guy in a donut shop. Their eyes meet across the room. Whenever Nancy glances in his direction he happens to be glancing back. It feels like magic.

He comes over. 'Mind if I join you?'

It's fine with her.

'Want another doney?' he asks her.

'A doney? Do you mean a donut?' she asks.

'Yeah.'

'No,' Nancy says, then remembers to be polite. 'No thank you.' That's the end of that.

Anyway, she doesn't want to get involved with anyone. Never again. She pats her belly, remembering what happened last time.

LETTERS FROM SARAH

Dear Fern,

In the park below my window a couple is dancing to music from a transistor radio, then pausing, just holding each other. They speak in silences. A tension holds them together, close, closer.

They don't know I watch, or else don't care.

I must do something to divert them. In a moment it will be too late.

Dear Fern,

Sometimes I think relationships are just a Freudian joke.

A man fondles a woman the way her father never could. He hugs her everywhere, inside and out. He is touching his mother, reaching back toward a womb he never wanted to leave.

The woman and man are not in love with one another, but her father and his mother keep on fucking.

Dear Fern,

Cottagers install purple outdoor lights for zapping insects. I needed something like that to zap my ugly thoughts. I suspected Martin of cheating right from the beginning, long before it actually happened. Zap zap. I should have incinerated that thought.

I needed some fool-proof test like diabetics use to check for sugar, a litmus stick to check his words for lies. But it was already too late: if I felt the need for a litmus test the trust was already gone. Without trust there's nothing.

He'd come home from a business trip. I'd greet him in a ruffled apron, faking it, the happy little housewife. 'Hi, dear. Have a nice trip?' He needed litmus paper too.

Dear Fern,

I tried to do everything right, probably tried too hard, loving phrases scattered about like knick-knacks, giving the apartment a cozy cluttered lived-in feel.

Action verbs stashed in the kitchen drawer with other utensils: cut, chop, clatter, thump, stutter, explain, explain, explain. Hot words on top of the stove: passion, incandescence, swelter, sultry. Cool ones stored in the fridge: chill, insensitive, shiver. Soft ones sprawled on the couch: dissolve, mollify, agree, appease, apologize, give in. Reconciliation at whatever price.

Words pulling at each other like magnets, determined to fasten together, whether they're suitable or not. Me hollering, 'Not so fast!' Dashing back and forth, handing out conjunctions and prepositions, and generally getting in the way.

Dear Fern,

There must be life beyond this planet. In this universe where perfection surrounds us, somewhere they must exist, the perfect ones, beyond the horizon of our awareness. There must be flying saucers and extraterrestrial life, or why do we exist? Without an audience there'd be no need for clowns.

Dear Fern,

I'm babbling. Don't read these. Throw them out.

PRENATAL CHECK-UP

'I finally went to see my doctor,' Nancy says.

Fern smiles. She has been pushing for this. 'How did it go?'

'It was okay. Kind of interesting, in fact. All the things I've been noticing are normal. I thought something was wrong because I'm peeing all the time, but it's just because the baby's pressing on my bladder. Maybe I'd have figured that out for myself if I'd known where my bladder was. And it's okay for me to be tired, and my breasts to hurt. He gave me a little booklet. All the same things happen to everyone.'

'Of course they do. Your body's got a lot of adjusting to do.'

'The doctor wants to do an ultrasound, but I'm not sure.'

'Why not?'

'They show you the baby on a screen. I'm not sure I want to see it. Sometimes I try to pretend this isn't happening, it's just a dream, and if I wait a little bit longer I'll finally wake up. I don't want to see a little caterpillar-slug actually squirming inside my belly. I'm not quite ready to face it. I keep thinking this is too grown-up a thing for me to be doing. I'm just a kid.'

All the same, now that Nancy has read her pregnancy pamphlet she suddenly wants to know a lot more. Libraries seem like nice places to hang out in anyway; they're pretty quiet and people leave you alone. She skims through one book after another about pregnancy, about taking care of babies. It's an obsession. She can't stop.

'Did you know they used ether in the old days?' she asks Fern. 'Women were unconscious. They didn't know anything until later on when it was all over and they woke up.'

'I remember when they changed to epidurals,' Fern says. 'Freezing injected into the spine. It made women numb from the waist down, so they couldn't feel any pain. But they could be awake, that was the great thing: the nurse would tilt a mirror, and a woman could watch her own baby being born.'

'Did you have one?'

'No, but I knew women who thought they were wonderful.'

'What about you? Were you asleep?'

'They put an ether mask within reach so I could take a whiff whenever I needed it. I must have used it. It's so long ago now I can't quite remember, but the twins were little and came pretty fast.'

'He wants me to come every month. I told him, sorry, I'm going to school, I don't have time.'

'It doesn't matter, Nancy. This is important. Don't fool around with your baby's health. You have to make time. That's that.'

'Yeah. The doctor said the same thing.'

NAMES

'When I had my babies there was a war on. Well, of course. There is always a war on somewhere.'

Fern is mumbling to herself again. Yammering, always yammering, she thinks, saying nothing, nothing important. When will it all stop? she wonders. Not yet, not yet.

While she and Nancy eat supper Fern tries to stay alert, pay attention, even chat. It is her apartment, she is the hostess after all. But afterward, while Nancy washes dishes, Fern sets her mind loose, free to wander back and forth in time, wherever it wants.

'But why?' she asks her mother. 'How'd you ever think of a name like that? Other girls are named after their grandmas and aunts and great aunts: they have ordinary names like Peggy or Patsy or Annie or Doris.' Fern is a child and asks her mother over and over, because she can't hear the answer often enough.

'Ordinary names are boring,' Mommy says. 'Those are old-fashioned names for women who stitch needlepoint samplers and crochet doilies, embroider pastel flowers on pillowslips. Anyone can have a plain old name like that. Fern is a beautiful outdoor name for someone special. The kind of person who pays attention to nature, who loves birds and butterflies and worms and insects, weeds and trees. Fern's a name that belongs in a forest. Green and sun-dappled and mysterious.'

'Did you ever visit a forest like that?' Fern asks.

'Just in picture books,' Mommy tells her. 'But maybe some day we'll go and explore those northern woods.'

Fern keeps waiting but it never happens.

A fly is buzzing around Fern's face. Which one? she wonders. Her ancient wrinkled eighty-year-old face or her smooth childhood one? But anyway, so what? What difference does it make? Fern waves her arms until it's gone.

October

HANLAN'S POINT

Nancy bursts through the door. 'Hey, Fernie. Guess what? We got our assignments back today. I got an A!'

'Fernie?'

'Oops. Sorry. It just slipped out. Do you mind much? It sounds kinda sweet. Undignified though, like a kid's name. Did your folks ever call you that when you were little?'

'Fernie! Where's Fernie?' The whole family is at Hanlan's Point for a picnic. Lemonade, hard-boiled eggs, peanut-butter sandwiches, potato salad.

Lots of grown-ups. Parents. Aunts and uncles, a doddering grandparent and great aunt, a teenaged cousin who ignores Fern and only wants to read a book. Adults keep reminiscing about some old days. 'It was better then,' they say again and again. 'Remember when...'

Fern, the only child, bored by adult conversation, tired of being ignored, finally wanders off, unnoticed. She hides behind some bushes, watches, wonders how soon they will notice her absence.

It takes a long time, but eventually people begin milling about, shading their eyes, peering in all directions, hollering, 'Fernie. Fernie. Hey, Fernie.'

What happened when they found her? Probably a bawling out, a spanking, some kind of public humiliation. Luckily she has blocked out that part.

Wasn't there an old roller-skating rink with a wooden floor? Or does she just remember her parents talking about it? She can almost remember watching the skaters whirling around and around, Fern becoming dizzy herself, mesmerized.

That picnic spot now buried beneath a runway.

Nancy is still awaiting suitable acknowledgement. A bit of enthusiasm would be nice. 'An A!' she says again. 'Isn't that amazing?'

DEAD FRIENDS

'Today was great,' Nancy says. 'We were so busy at school I forgot about being pregnant.'

'Pregnant?' Fern says. 'You're pregnant? Really? I didn't know that.'

Nancy stares at her, mouth agape.

'I was trying to be funny,' Fern reassures her. 'You know, making conversation.' It didn't work though. If she ever knew how to kid around she has forgotten.

'I'm exhausted,' Nancy says. 'I think I'll go to bed right after supper.'

What am *I* supposed to do? Fern wonders. Who's going to talk to *me*? Entertain *me*?

'Don't you have any friends? Folks you could visit, who could come and visit you?'

Fern realizes she must have spoken aloud. Oh no. This isn't the first time it's happened; there's no chance it'll be the last.

'Dead,' Fern says. 'Dead, or else in nursing homes already and might as well be. A couple of healthy ones moved down to Florida. That's the trouble with being eighty. There's no one left.'

'Too bad. There's probably some great people in this apartment building. I wonder how you could get to know them.'

Next day Fern does the laundry even though not much needs washing. It seems like a good meeting place.

REVOLVING DOORS

'All of life is a bunch of doors revolving,' says Fern to whoever bothers to listen in the laundry room of the apartment building. 'All my life has been doors revolving,' she repeats, trying to seem profound, being mistaken for senile by people waiting for their clothes to wash or tumble dry, reading paperbacks and magazines, trying to ignore her.

Fern's mind wanders backward into the past. Younger, younger. A dawdling dreamer of a child, she is dragged downtown on shopping trips to Eaton's and Simpson's, shoved inside a revolving door, she and her mother squashed into the same section, her mother's purse squeezed against her head, Fern skipping awkwardly to keep her balance while her mother pushes the door forward. They both burst forth a moment later, propelled into the perfume department or jewellery or clocks.

Fern keeps getting bigger. Now her mother strides on ahead, disappears through revolving glass into one department store or the other, and then waits, tapping her foot, impatient to paw through remnants and pattern books, to try on one pair of shoes after another before deciding none of them are exactly right.

Fern on the outside, staring at that terrible door, watching one person after another move through it. Knowing she should be able to do this. Even then she was such a disappointment to herself.

Finally her mother comes outside again, grabs Fern, and forces her into a section of the door, Fern's feet scrabbling to keep her balance as the glass door shoves at her back. Finally though she is inside the store, safe, intact, but not for long. She'll have to face that door again to get back out.

Her mother has to price everything three times: Simpson's, followed by Eaton's, then she and Fern hurry along the tunnel to Eaton's Annex, her mother keeping her head down so no one will see her and realize she's poor. The hallway smells of waffles and fast food, a lovely aroma. It reminds Fern of the carnival that moves into the park for a week each summer and changes it into a bright colourful fairyland. While the carnival is there Fern always forgets what the park used to look like, forgets it is even the same place at all. Then one morning she wakes up from her carnival dream and discovers everything has disappeared. No rides, no tents, no music or side-shows or coloured lights. Even the popcorn smell is gone. Candy wrappers litter the ground. Nothing else remains.

On the way to Eaton's Annex, Fern always slows down by the waffle display and tugs at her mother's dress, 'Please, Mommy.' 'You can't be hungry again,' her mother says, 'not after that big breakfast.' Breakfast? Fern can't remember eating breakfast. Or else her mother says, 'Not today. I can't afford it,' as if on some other day she could. They pass children whose mothers can afford it, who don't care whether their children's faces are smeared with grease or ice cream or chocolate, children who have been trusted to stay right there and eat their treats and not get into trouble while their parents finish shopping. Those children are having a great time. They race back and forth, dodging the big blue warehouse carts that roll through the tunnel from one store to the other. Those carts scare Fern, the rumbling sound coming closer and closer, until the racket of the wheels on bare floors is louder than the rumble of Fern's stomach wanting ice cream inside a waffle, a man's voice hollering just behind her, 'Watch the cart, please! Watch the cart.'

Her mother grabs Fern's hand and drags her like a baby, quickly, past waffle vendors and laughing children. Suddenly Fern has a glimpse of how the rest of her childhood will be: no matter how old she gets, Mommy will never allow her to play and get dirty and have fun.

Fern yanks her hand loose. 'All right then,' says Mommy, 'I won't hold your hand if you keep up. I don't want to have to go looking for you at the Lost and Found. Not today. I don't have time.'

Would she bother to look? Fern wonders. If Fern was turned in like a lost parcel or umbrella, how long would it take for her mother to come?

Sometimes they ride on an elevator and Fern has to watch out for two sets of doors. A solid door and an accordion one with metal diamonds that collapse and fold together, like the wooden gate fastened at the top of the cellar stairs so her little brother won't fall down them and break his neck. A woman slides both sets of doors open and shut. She wears a dark dress with white collar and cuffs, and looks official, like a policeman. She calls out floor numbers and all the merchandise in the store, talking non-stop. 'Fourth floor. Furniture and carpets. Anyone for four? Step back and let them out please. The doors are closing. Watch the doors. Going up. Fifth floor. Fine china, bedding, children's toys. Anyone else for five? The doors are closing. Watch the doors.'

The store is made for giants. The counter tops are as high as the top of Fern's head.

Towels are on sale, crowds of people clustered thick around the table. Fern is crushed by cloth coats and fat hips, and a man who shouts, 'Just a minute. I think there's someone down here. Bless my soul. Indeed there is. It looks like a little girl. What's your name, sweetie?' Fern tells him, and then her mother grabs her by the hand and yanks her away. 'Haven't I told you never to talk to strange men? You've no more sense than a squirrel.' They head for ladies' gloves.

Fern watches leather fingers cover her mother's shiny red nails. Then her mother works at the leather, pulling it up slowly, covering each finger, until finally her whole hand disappears, becomes black and smooth and mysterious.

Then they are back at the revolving door, Mommy already out on Queen Street again, turning around, calling, 'Hurry up. A street-car's coming,' seeing Fern waiting inside the store, watching the door spin as other people pass through it. Then Mommy is inside the store again, grabbing her, yanking her into a section of the door, Fern squished by all the parcels, finally scooting out onto Queen Street, safe, grinning up at her mother for a split second, then cringing back, because Mommy is angry again, the streetcar's gone, they'll be late starting Poppa's supper, the next streetcar's crowded, not like the one they missed which Mommy says had lots of space. They have to stand up all the way to Woodbine.

Anyway, she had survived the door again, her melton cloth coat clutched tight against her body, for fear the hem might catch behind her as she dashed in, pulling the door to a sudden halt, or, even worse, it could get caught behind her as she dashes out, yank-ing her backward off her feet, or her sleeve caught, pulling her arm right out of its socket, whatever that means. Fern tries not to imag-ine what an arm socket is, her arm suddenly unscrewed like a light bulb, her on the outside of the store staring down at her empty absence of arm, of sleeve, looking up, seeing it lying on the ground inside a section of revolving door, with old cigarette butts and crum-pled newspapers, getting more and more filthy, spinning around for-ever on the tiny circle of pavement.

A neighbour has an empty coat sleeve. Poppa says his arm was lost at war. Lost. How could he possibly lose it?

'Wash your hands,' Mommy always says before supper. Would she change it to, 'Wash your hand?' And how would Fern ever man-age to anyway? Surely Mommy would have to scrub it for her, or be satisfied if Fern just gave it a good soak.

The streetcar jerks. Fern grabs her mother's coat with both hands and hangs on tight.

HOTSHOT

Nancy stares at children in a playground and wonders who her baby will look like, herself or Brad. A baby that resembles its daddy would be a constant reminder. She doesn't want that. Even though Brad's cute, has hotshot style.

Brad wears his hair just so, covering his eyes, the way teachers and parents hate. He struts through crowds, shoves right through them like the honour guard at some parade.

And he seems like Santa Claus to Nancy and every other girl he meets; he's a rock singer or movie star or marching band, whatever marvel she reads about in the newspaper each day, or hears on radio, sees on TV. Teenaged girls should line the streets to twirl batons, cheer, turn cartwheels as he struts by.

Brad has style. Nancy used to watch him and wonder why she was such a sucker for it.

That hotshot hair style no one liked, she tried to change it once when he was half-asleep and didn't notice. But he turned into someone else when she brushed back his hair. A stranger's grey marble eyes looked out at her from fifteen icy million miles away. A person with eyes like that would stomp her like an ant, would roll like chariot wheels over anyone they didn't like, and those hard eyes would not like anyone. They'd glare and glare till everyone was gone, and maybe then they'd almost smile.

Brad has style, but only when he wears his hair just so, covering his eyes, the way teachers and parents don't like, but he does, and also Nancy.

Brad. She still misses him like a pulled tooth, still reaches out toward him, iron filing yanked toward a magnet. Does he still look the same? She has no idea.

LETTERS FROM SARAH

Dear Fern,

I haven't found the butterflies yet, haven't found true happiness and peace and serenity either. Haven't even been looking. Not yet. I'm still in boring London thinking about my past, trying to sort it out.

But I'm no different from all the other women I know. We compare notes. 'How are you?' someone asks, and then they tell; they've just been waiting for someone to show a bit of interest. They think their mates take them for granted. They've begun to feel like cooks and cleaning women, and suspect they're being used. Handy, expendable, easily discarded like socks tossed in a corner. Their spouses stay late at the office, have lost interest in sex. Could they be getting it on with other partners? Well, of course. Why not? Younger women are everywhere, mysterious, attractive, with university degrees and interesting jobs. They have travelled to far-off places, can talk of a fascinating outside world instead of the same old trite domestic patter.

We wait in turn for our sad drab co-workers to stop and take a breath so we can tell them our lives are the same.

We lean on relationships these days the way our ancestors depended on religion. There must be more to life than this, we keep thinking. Life's beginning to lose its meaning and it must be someone's fault. At first we blame ourselves. Later on we blame our mates, even though they're victims too.

Men keep trying to find out who they are. They are thirty or sixty-five and still don't know. We women don't understand. After all men never even had to change their names. I know, I know. Women don't have to either. We know this in our minds but some of us don't believe it in our hearts, aren't sure we can get away with it. Will men still marry us if we insist on keeping our own names?

Why am I ranting on and on about this? I never got married anyway, didn't want a ball-and-chain commitment, and neither did Martin. No piece of paper was going to be the thing keeping us together. Nothing would do that but love. Love, sweet love. Lust by another name.

But eventually love's not enough. People get tired. Working at a relationship takes too much energy. Men pack up and move on, try to discover the meaning of their existence. It turns out they have to find a different partner in order to do this. Women try to be understanding. We humour them, wish them well, hope it's just some phase they're going through, like children who pass through one stage and then another while trying to grow up.

Men move away. We watched our fathers do it, thinking, this is what men are like. If my father can do this, so will any other man. The sons watched too. 'This is what we men are like,' they told each other. 'Some day we'll walk out too.'

Self-fulfilling prophecies.

I was the one who told Martin to leave. I keep forgetting.

PEPPERMINT

A woman shoves a shopping cart into the laundry room and drags a crying child behind her. 'Stand still and don't move,' she orders, and then begins shoving clothes into a washer. She turns around once and yells at the child, 'Shut up. Stop that bawling.'

'What's your name, sweetie?' Fern asks, offering the child a peppermint candy.

'Get away from my kid,' the woman hollers. 'What are you? Some kind of weirdo? Some kind of nut?'

LONG-TERM COMMITMENT

'Omigod, Fern. I just realized I'll have to eat healthy for a lot longer than I thought. Not just until this little grub gets out of my belly, but while it's little, while it's watching me and learning about the world. No smoking. No living on junk food. I'll have to set a good example. I want my baby to grow up strong.'

'Also you need to be healthy yourself, so you'll have lots of energy, be able to cope.'

'I guess.'

'And so you'll be here, so you'll be alive while the child is growing up.'

'But that's nearly twenty years!'

'Yes. A generation.'

'No more cigarettes for twenty years! No more fries with gravy! It's not fair. I'd never bargained for that.'

POEM

Fern finds a poem in a magazine and cuts it out, even though it seems silly to do this, because every day she dumps another drawer full of possessions into plastic grocery bags and tosses them down the garbage chute.

old winter woman

an old woman and cat
stare at winter through a window

time squeezes through the
hourglass of sky

hours hover   giant snowflakes
each slightly different
but they seem the same

days roll together   soft as
silver mercury   silently
swallow each other into weeks

months layer upon each other
a soft pillow she can lie on
and dream that she is young

Why does she bother to save it? she wonders. She doesn't even have a cat.

She shows it to Nancy, who gives it a quick glance, 'Oh yeah, very nice,' then continues working on some assignment.

'It deserves more attention than that,' Fern says. Meaning: me. I deserve more attention.

FETAL MOVEMENTS

'Wow, Fern. Guess what? I can feel the baby moving!'

'Really? You're that far along?'

'Five months. It's supposed to happen around now. But actually I've been feeling this off and on for a week or two. I just didn't realize what it was. This time I'm sure.'

'Can I feel it? Do you mind?'

Nancy places Fern's hand in the right place but by then the baby has drifted back to sleep.

'Do you feel different? Does it make the baby seem more real?'

'Well, yeah. You bet. Now I know there's really something in there. Not a tapeworm. Something human. Someone's alive, living right inside me. It's pretty weird.'

Poor little thing, Nancy thinks. Groping in darkness. Wondering, where am I? How did I get here? Wanting to explore this place, learn and understand it. Floundering around, trying to swim like a little goldfish, but always bumping into womb walls.

Lucky little infant, Fern thinks. Nancy's going to be a wonderful parent. She's a natural. Child-rearing's going to be instinctive. Nancy will manage. She and her youngster will do just fine.

AGES

Fern's mind wanders back and forth in time, aimless. Fifteen years old. Sixty. Twenty-five. She lingers at fifty, at last alone. Walter gone, the twins gone too. Sometimes she almost misses that busy childhood time, but then remembers how frenzied her life was and decides not.

In her twenties. Preparing supper. Ten to six. Time frozen like vegetables. Twin toddlers underfoot, banging saucepan lids together. Fern frantic, dashing back and forth, tripping over them. Rushing toward the six o'clock deadline when Walter walks in the door, sits down at the table, waits for food to be set in front of him. Afterward she scours supper dishes and pots and pans and children, stacking them away until tomorrow. Did she ever take time to enjoy her husband, her daughters? She can't remember.

Then fifty years old, alone at last. Ten to six, and the house is silent, Fern wondering why she was always in such a rush, and what she missed.

Fifty! She'd expected to be wiser, to have somehow assimilated, learned, developed, but apparently not yet. Fern is only half a century. She still has time.

Fern is sixty-five, seventy. Is it possible? She stares inside a mirror at a stranger's sagging breasts and wrinkled neck. She wants her own smooth young body back again. This time she'll appreciate it.

She bargains with whoever's out there, promises to do anything it wants, relive her past, make changes, in order to be thirty, forty, fifty again. Any age but this one, which keeps changing as she bargains.

Eighty. Can she be really be eighty already?

'I don't feel any different.' She talks aloud, telling the walls, or else Nancy, if Nancy's at home and paying attention. 'I still feel so young, as though I'm in the middle of my life.'

Perhaps people comment to each other, 'Isn't she amazing!' Fern's sure they must. She certainly hopes so.

Fern is old though. She knows it.

Once Fern was a teenager. She remembers those empty wasteland years, just putting in time. She seemed to be mostly missing, an absence of this, a lack of that, always impatient to grow older, wanting the next stage, whatever it was, to hurry up and begin. Her future, those golden blissful years, always just ahead, tantalizing, unattainable, somewhere beyond her next birthday: a time when she would be happy, fulfilled, fit comfortably inside the world around her, when she would have self-confidence, majestic impressive breasts, and clothes that would draw attention to them, when she would think substantial thoughts, ones that mattered and were original and stunned strangers with their insight.

But it doesn't happen. She grows old instead, her past becoming a heavier and heavier burden she drags behind her, wanting to shed.

Other things happened too.

Fern is in her mid-twenties; her pregnancy is behind her. She has her babies, twin daughters. All three of them have survived the childbirth ordeal. Fern can hardly believe it. 'Look at their little fingers,' she says to Walter, 'their tiny toes.' She counts to ten over and over. Her babies are perfect. Good, because Fern never intends to go through that again.

Sweet little baby mouths are always open. They already know how to wail.

'Do something,' Walter says. 'Feed them or something.'

'I'm exhausted,' Fern tells him. 'I gave them birth. It's your turn. Take them out for a walk in the carriage.'

Walter phones his mother to come and help out.

Fern is sixty years old and still thinks she's in the middle of her life. She has always thought this.

Or Fern is seventeen. Her future stretches before her. She might live until she's thirty at the most. Well, of course she can't actually imagine being as old as thirty, but most people do live that long. Are they able to imagine what it will be like ahead of time, she wonders, being so old, being mature? Is it only her who can't imagine that far ahead? Only her with some brain deficiency, an absence of whatever part of the brain is capable of such imaginings. Another lack. Brain lack. Among all the other lacks: beauty, grace, intellect, dazzling conversation. Whatever.

Fern is into her twenties now and pregnant. She can't wait to have a baby, can't wait for someone to love her and be dependent, to need her so much they would die if she wasn't there.

Maybe Walter will love her better if she has a baby.

Or maybe Walter will love her later on when she is thin again, not pregnant, when she can bend over to tie her shoes.

Fern is in the delivery room. 'Two,' the doctor tells her.

Fern can hardly hear him; she's still crying, and a baby is bawling inside this room. 'Too what?'

'Twins. Both girls, though. Too bad. Men like boys better. Maybe next time. Anyway they seem fine. Two healthy baby girls.'

Next time? Fern thinks he must be kidding.

'Twins?' asks Walter. 'Are you sure? Oh no! We can't afford them.'

Fern is old now and wonders where her life went. All those years. Whatever happened during them? Not much. She did not change the world. She did not matter much to anyone except family and a few friends. She invented nothing, never had an original thought; no one, neither parents nor husband nor daughters, ever gazed at her in awe and wonder. She didn't dazzle like the stars, or even birthday candles. But sometimes she almost felt the darkness flicker. Perhaps that should be enough. It will have to be enough.

ST. MARGARET'S IN THE PINES

It is a Saturday in October. Indian summer weather. Fern and Nancy wear heavy jackets just in case.

They are in a cemetery in Scarborough behind a church. St. Margaret's in the Pines. Fern picked it because of the name.

'You know, Fern, eighty isn't so old. One of my classmates has a greatgrandma who's almost ninety, and she still plays bridge and euchre and beats people who are younger. She belongs to some kind of social club for seniors and goes there every afternoon.'

Fern changes the subject. 'What did he say when you told him?'

'Brad?'

'The father. Yes.'

'He doesn't know.'

'But...'

'I lied to you about it. I never told him. I don't intend to.'

Silence.

'Well, why should I? If he knows he'll feel he has to be involved. See it once in a while. Cuddle it. Get to brag and haul out baby pictures.'

'Sooner or later he'll find out you're pregnant.'

'I'll lie. I'll say the father was someone else.'

'I don't know about that. Are you're certain you'll never want to get back together?'

'Never. Absolutely not. We had something special and then he threw it away. It's all over. We broke up last winter, right after Christmas.'

Fern is silent. Nancy knows she's doing the math.

'Well, okay. Yeah. We tried to get back together last spring but it didn't work. He rushed too much. I guess he thought we could just pick up where we left off. Go to bed again right away. I didn't want it, Fern. I needed to be wooed a bit.'

'Was it rape?'

'Not really, but I said no and he wasn't listening, didn't pay attention. I didn't want it, but he was in too much of a hurry to notice or even care. It wasn't rape, not exactly, because he didn't mean it that way, but it was as close as I ever want to get. I was struggling and it hurt.'

'The trouble is...' Fern begins, and then she stops.

'What?'

'Never mind.'

'No. Tell me. Be straight with me. You're the only person I ever talk to about anything important.'

'Well, have you thought about the child in this?'

'Fern! What are you talking about? You know me. I'm practically obsessed. I think about this baby all the time! What it will look like, how much I'll love it, all the things I need to learn in order to take good care of it.'

'That's not what I mean. Doesn't the child have a right to know its father? Not to live with him, but to have some kind of relationship?'

'I'll be there for this child all the time. One hundred per cent. Having a mother who's committed will be enough.' Nancy walks off to bring an end to the conversation, but pretty soon she comes back again. 'Will it hurt, Fern? How much? Am I going to be able to stand it?'

'You'll be all right. There's no point me saying it won't hurt. You wouldn't believe me. Labour contractions hurt but you'll be able to cope.'

Fern tries to be reassuring, but remembers all too well when the twins were born. The whole experience wasn't beautiful at all, her screaming, wanting to be stoical, but screaming anyway. If only she could have held them for a moment afterward, but the twins were rushed right to the nursery and closed up inside incubators. Brisk efficient nurses provided whatever was needed, warned Fern, 'Shhh. Just look. Be quiet. Don't touch, don't touch.'

'Anyway,' she continues, 'they'll give you pain medication if you want it. If they don't offer it, don't be afraid to ask. Don't feel you've got to prove how strong you are. You don't need to be the bravest patient they've ever had. They don't care.'

Has she been reassuring? Has she said enough? 'There'll be pain, but it's forgotten the moment it's over.' There. Fern repeats that same old lie all women tell.

While remembering, reliving the birth pains, still feeling guilty after all these years for having screamed and screamed and screamed.

LETTERS FROM SARAH

Dear Fern,

Losses are forever. Twice I had a baby inside my belly. The first was given up for adoption, and the second died inside me. Nothing helped then, or ever since.

Martin mourned the last one with me, or tried to, but it wasn't the same for him. He hadn't felt the baby inside his belly, shifting position, kicking his bladder. He hadn't whispered secrets to it when no one was around, sung lullabies, told stories, described all the wonders of the great world outside the womb: butterflies and ladybugs, rain puddles, snow angels. Kicking through dry leaves in the fall, scrunching through snow in winter...

How could it die? But how could it start growing in the first place? That never seemed possible either.

Dear Fern,

I intended to be a perfect mother. I knew I could do it, and nothing else in the world could possibly be more important. I played beautiful music on a walkman, the headphones propped against my belly: Mozart, Bach, Beethoven, Brahms. Not Vivaldi though, because I'd read that babies found it disturbing.

The things we do for our kids. The sacrificing had started already. Because I didn't even like classical music myself. Such a small concession though, and I was happy to make it. 'Enjoy,' I told my child. 'This is just a small sample of how beautiful your world will be. Enjoy. Rest up. Relax.'

I even read to it about contractions, about birth, soothing the child as best I could, 'I know, I know, it sounds bad, but it's better for you to know what to expect. Anyway, don't worry. We'll get through it together. Other mothers and babies do. I'll think about finally being able to hold you in my arms, cuddling you, suckling; you can think about all the wonders of the world just waiting for you to explore.'

It sounds crazy now. Maybe pregnancy makes you a little daft.

Then I'd hear Martin's key in the door, his footsteps heading for the kitchen, hoping for supper. Supper! I'd forgotten all about it. I'd grab the headphones and move them up to my own ears.

Martin framed in the bedroom doorway, staring down at the bed. 'You all right?'

'Yeah, sure. Just listening to some music.'

He reached for the headphones. 'An orchestra? I didn't think you liked long-hair stuff.'

'Yeah. Well...'

My mind already drifting elsewhere, daydreaming of baby names. Maybe Ella Marie if it's a girl, after my sweet grandmas. If only they were alive and could see me now, could know their little Sarah was going to become a mother, that they'd have a great-grandchild to share, to take turns pushing its carriage to the park. 'This is the best thing you've ever done,' they'd tell me, 'the best present you could give us.'

Or thinking I'd maybe name the child for my mother. Myrna. Even women who never cuddled their own kids sometimes go crazy over grandchildren. I'd read a magazine article about this. It gave me a headache. Life's so unfair.

My mother pulling out her wallet on a cruise ship. 'Wanta see my grandkid?' she'd ask whichever guy was buying drinks tonight. One snapshot after another. Baby Myrna chewing a rattle. Baby Myrna sound asleep, a teddy bear propped beside her. 'I bought her that teddy bear and frilly shawl,' Myrna would tell him. 'Also a stroller. Perego. The salesclerk said they're the best.' The guy would stare at Myrna in amazement. Who'd have thought it? This is a side of Myrna he's never seen before. Underneath her hard-boiled manner she's really rather sweet. He reaches his arm across the table, runs his finger around her lips. 'Let's get out of here, sugar. Let's walk on the deck and count stars.'

Martin, back in the bedroom again. How much time has gone past? This time turning the walkman off, saying, 'What about supper?'

'Supper? Oh yeah.'

This baby. All the dreams and needs of parents and grandparents would have to be met by this one small person. Do babies know about the heavy responsibility they bear? No wonder they scream so much.

I imagined Martin in the hospital, holding the baby awkwardly, pacing back and forth along the corridor. 'This place is a hospital,' he'd tell it. 'Pretty boring, eh? No teddy bears. No mobiles fluttering above your bed. But just wait-'ll you get home. We'll show what the good life can be like. Winnie the Pooh and Tigger and Kanga are waiting on the wall beside your crib.'

The baby listening, thinking, nothing but talk, talk, talk. Where's the music? She promised me classical music.

That sweet little infant died inside me, no one knows why. The doctors had to induce labour so it would come out.

Dear Fern,

Did you ever hear from the young woman with blue hair? The one who looked pregnant. Nancy? Was that her name? I was so jealous of her. Do you suppose she had any idea how lucky she was? Probably not. A fetus growing and changing inside her, like a butterfly passing through all its chrysalis changes.

A-YUL

Two o'clock in the morning, Nancy hears voices, peers out the apartment window.

'So long, Al,' a woman calls, slowly, pronouncing both *long* and *Al* with two syllables: 'So lo-ong, A-yul,' all southern and sexy. Her words hang suspended on the humid air. She leans over a balcony railing in the next building, backlit by the light from the window behind her.

Other windows in the building are dark. Occupants sleep, probably tossing now, a bit restless now that the words, 'So lo-ong, A-yul' have entered their dreams.

But the frowzy blonde doesn't care. She is smiling, sleepy-eyed, probably post-orgasmic. She wears a cotton wrapper, and leans her soft bulging body against the balcony railing as she watches him walk toward the streetcar stop.

A good-time woman, Nancy thinks. Good-time. A phrase her mother might have used. Nancy can't believe she thought that word.

The woman calls it again, 'So lo-ong, A-yul,' a little louder this time, because Al has moved farther away.

Why doesn't she shut up? Nancy wonders. Doesn't she realize people are trying to sleep?

Look at her; she is nothing. Look at him; he's nothing too. His hair combed so the few remaining strands stretch across his bald spot. He looks seedy, trousers bagging at the seat. If he had the money to buy good clothes he wouldn't know how to pick them out.

Why am I being so nasty? Nancy wonders. What do I care about this tacky couple? Oh no! Surely I'm not jealous.

At the corner Al turns back toward the woman, grins, blows her a kiss. She blows one back, then begins singing an old schmaltzy love song, 'Younger than springtime am I...' Oh no, Nancy thinks, what next? Nancy remembers the song from some movie video her mother had insisted she watch, a love story of course.

Back in bed she tosses and turns, yearning for Brad, or some man, any man. Imagining his hands touching her all over. Love, she thinks. Yuck! Why don't song-writers ever write about something else?

The song continues playing on and on inside her mind; she resists the urge to sing along.

PHONE CALL

'Thanksgiving's coming up,' Fern says. 'A family day. A good time to bury the hatchet. You ought to phone your folks. They must be worried about you.'

'Not a chance.'

Fern persists though, mentioning it every morning at break-fast. 'You're not the only one inside this crisis. Your parents are involved. They have feelings too. They've had some time to think things over and now perhaps they've changed their minds. Also something could be wrong. Someone in your family could be sick and you wouldn't know.'

Finally, 'I'll phone them if you'll call the twins.'

'You go first.'

'Daddy? This is Nancy.'

Click. Dial tone. Nancy's face blanches as though she's been slapped. 'Screw them! I don't care!' she hollers, heading outside for a walk, quick, before Fern can notice the tears.

Next morning Fern answers the phone. 'Hello.' Silence. 'Hello?'

Finally a woman's voice, 'Is Nancy there?'

'No. Who is this?'

Click.

A few days later the woman phones again.

'Nancy's at school. Can she phone you back?'

'No. It'll just make trouble. I'm Nancy's mother. Is she all right?'

'Finally. What took you so long?'

'The other night while her daddy was busy I called the phone company number, the code that tells which was the last number that called. Her father doesn't know I have this phone number. He'd be furious if he knew I'd called.'

'So you have a pathetic relationship with your bossy husband. So what? I couldn't care less. Nancy's the only person who matters right now. Do you care about your daughter or not?'

'Of course. That's why I phoned. Is she all right?'

'You mean, physically? Is she healthy? I think so. She went for a check-up.'

'Is she happy?'

'You kick her out, your own daughter, at the time when she needs you most, and then have the nerve to ask if she's happy!' Fern slams down the phone.

But it rings again right away. 'I'll keep phoning and pestering until I find out,' Nancy's momma says. 'I want to see her but her daddy still refuses. Ross is having a lot of trouble with this. He still thinks she's a little girl.'

'HIS little girl. Fathers are all the same. They never want their little princesses to grow up and fall in love with some other man. They want to keep their daughters pure and virginal forever, their hymens always intact.'

'Don't say things like that. Her daddy's a nice man.'

'It doesn't matter. All fathers are the same. It's probably normal. Anyway, that's not what's important. This is a crisis. Get working on him non-stop and bring him around. Get him to a counsellor and hurry up about it. Nancy needs parents, and her child's going to need grandparents. I'm too old. I can't hang around long enough.'

'He thinks she should marry the boy.'

'He got to marry whoever he wanted. She has the same right.'

'Well, not exactly. It wasn't that simple. I was pregnant with Nancy. It was shotgun. We had to get married.'

'Oh.'

'Twenty years ago, and we've managed, but just barely. On the whole they've been pretty good years. But now it's happening all over again and this time it's even worse because we can't control it. Nancy doesn't care what we think.'

'Well, if you'd just...'

'It's on his mind all the time. Just eating him up. Twenty years! Our whole life together. It's like it was wasted, means nothing. If she doesn't have to marry the boy, then maybe we didn't have to get married either. Her daddy would have been able to finish law school. He'd be the lawyer just as he and his parents had always dreamed of. Both our lives would have been completely different.

Who knows what they might have been like. All that angst and turmoil. It's mid-life crisis time anyway.'

'You should tell her. Explain.'

'Are you crazy? Tell her she wasn't wanted? That she forced us to settle for each other? I can't tell her that.'

'Don't phrase it that way. But you should tell her. Let her understand why you're both upset. She has a right.'

'No. Of course not. I can't. No way.'

Fern slams down the receiver, then yanks the jack from the wall to keep the woman from calling back. So there!

November

UNLEAVING

Fern stares out the window, watches leaves fall off the trees, smothering the ground.

Unleaving. A nice word from some old poem. Who in the world wrote it? Hopkins maybe. The trees more beautiful unleaved: her opinion, no one else's. So what? If other folks agreed, then she'd probably change her mind.

Fern stares at bare branches, envying their simplicity, their purity and grace. She remembers chemo patients in the hospital. At first she couldn't look at them but eventually came to appreciate the stark beauty of their bare skulls. Perfect, like marble sculptures by Barbara Hepworth or Henry Moore.

Fern plays only music on the radio. Whenever an announcer begins to speak she switches the dial. She has heard too many words already, enough to last her the rest of her life.

She has spoken too many of them herself, wasting them on her children when they were little, crooning, chanting nonsense rhymes, telling bedtime stories, always trying to lull them off to sleep. At the time nothing was more important, to make it possible for her to finally flop down on the couch herself.

Fern reaches her arms out, almost feels a hospital nurse place the babies inside them. 'They're big enough now. Take them home.' Pure bliss at first, having no idea what she was getting into.

Holding them, not wanting ever to let go. Holding on, for their sakes, to keep them safe. Also for her sake, but she still hasn't quite figured that one out. Maybe to make sense of her marriage and her life, justify her existence on this planet. Finally, finally, she has accomplished something useful.

They're already three weeks old when she is allowed to take them home. Surely she must have held them in the nursery, but no, she doesn't think so, can't remember. No wonder the magic mother-child bonding never took place. Possibly it's a myth anyway, only happens in how-to books, instructions for raising happy well-adjusted children. Those pious books, noble and well-meaning. She is tired all the time, too exhausted to bother reading library books, to pay attention to so much good advice. One more thing to feel guilty about.

Fern spends the first few years trying to get those babies to sleep, rocking back and forth, back and forth, in a darkened room, one baby and then the other. They are so beautiful when they're finally asleep, breath fluttering faint as moth wings, their chubby fists unclenched, their heads adrift inside swaddled baby dreams of nipples and milk, or whatever dreams babies fall into. 'Rest up,' she whispers, 'and keep growing,' because she'd always heard babies only grow while they're asleep.

Then Fern flops down to grab some shut-eye too, quick, while she has the chance.

Sometimes she sits and stares at them in love and wonder, but only when they're asleep. Once they wake up she's soon exhausted, irritable, snapping at them.

Days, weeks, months. Time seems to drag on and on forever, but all the same, before she knows it, those baby years are gone.

Then chatter, chatter, chatter: the busy toddler times. Fern talking all the time, giving too many words away. Why does she bother? Her children don't listen and nobody else does either. She should save her voice, store words in a paper bag, so she can reach in, grab a few whenever they're needed, fasten them together, sometimes this way, sometimes that. 'You remember...' 'I've told you and told you...' 'Listen! Pay attention...' 'Look both ways before you step off the sidewalk,' 'Don't put that in your mouth. It's dirty.'

Talking. Filling in all the empty gaps so she won't have time to think.

Once Fern was a baby herself, she must have been, her eyes unfocused, the world a blur of light and sound. Watching. Listening. Those noises, what are they? Voices of mother and father, roar of vacuum cleaner, clatter of pots and pans, dishes and cutlery. Baby Fern begins babbling herself, copying words, probably trying to mimic, 'Shut up, shut up,' the first words she remembers hearing.

BIRTHING CLASSES

'I'm supposed to be attending childbirth classes.'

'Well then, get going.'

'I keep putting it off because I'm scared to go alone, but my doctor nags me about it. All the others will be in couples. Do you suppose you could come with me?'

'Isn't there someone else you'd prefer? What about your mother? Why don't you phone her?'

'No.'

'A girlfriend? Someone from school?'

'Never mind. I don't want to go anyway.'

Emotional blackmail. Fern knows this, recognizes it from using it so often herself. But it doesn't matter. Nancy needs to go, to learn whatever can be taught beforehand. If Fern had known enough ahead of time she wouldn't have had her babies at all, but Nancy hasn't that option any longer; she's already six months along.

'Well, I could give it a try. It might be kind of interesting.'

'Oh never mind, Fern. It was just a thought. I'm getting fed up with being pregnant anyway. It's getting boring. And I hate all the disgusting side-effects. Indigestion and gas. I'm always farting. Don't pretend you haven't noticed.'

'Let's go once then. If you don't like it we won't go back.'

'See. It bothers you too. You're just too polite to mention it.'

HOSPITAL HALLWAY

Fern wakes up and can hardly see. She forgot to close the curtains last night and sun is streaming through the east window, blinding her eyes. Like the hospital, she thinks, remembering, even though she tries not to.

A memory, seared on her eyeballs: a hospital hall.

The hallway is too bright. Even through blurred cataracts Fern is aware of too many people walking too fast. They wear lab coats and coloured uniforms, name-tags with photographs, their names printed underneath, too small to read. Assorted voices, the rustle of crisp uniforms, the click of footsteps against tile floors. Brisk people, busy.

Not like Fern, not like all the doddering patients who totter back and forth, mumbling, their clothes askew, feet shuffling in paper slippers, the women's stockings rippling around their ankles. The frailest are lined up across from the nursing station, tied in wheelchairs, pleading to be put back into bed. Their heads tip over when they fall asleep.

The nurses tell Fern to get some exercise, walk back and forth along those halls, but Fern has watched tigers pace zoo cages and she refuses. She stays in bed, and keeps the blinds down so people can hardly see her, not notice how old and scrawny she has become.

Nurses talk to her loudly, slowly as though she's stupid. 'Remission,' is the cheery word they use. They manage to tell her something's in remission without ever saying the awful cancer word. They avoid the word and think they've fooled her. 'Isn't that nice?' they tell her. 'You don't need to be in hospital any longer, can go to a nursing home instead.' 'No,' Fern says. 'Of course not. I'm going home to my own house. I need to work on my garden. How long have I been here anyway? What month is this?'

They phone her daughters to come and tell her.

When she gets out of this hospital and feels stronger Fern plans to go walking in a forest. Other ferns will surround her. She will watch carefully and pay attention because there are so many different kinds. In a pocket of her purse she keeps a yellowed piece of paper that lists them. She unfolds it now, reads words aloud: *bracken, chain, cinnamon... The cliffbrakes, the spleenworts, the woodferns.* Fern likes the double words best: *crested shield, dissected grape, hart's tongue, silvery glade.* There are so many: *marsh, oak, ostrich, rattlesnake... Northern beech* and *northern holly. Polypody*: a word she can't even pronounce. So many, so many.

Some day she intends to study ferns, learn to identify them by the subtle pattern variations of their fronds. She'd better not put it off much longer. So far she has been imagining them instead. There are so many shades of green inside the parks and woodlands of her mind.

Some ferns live longer than humans. But Fern is feeling ancient these days, eighty years old now, most of a century. Beat that, plants, she thinks. Just try to beat that.

She would grow ferns in her back yard but it's too sunny. Woodsy plants deserve more privacy and shade than she can offer.

Her daughters come to visit, reluctant, and confess that her house and back yard are gone.

TOO BUSY

'Which evening is that childbirth class?' Fern asks. 'We don't want to miss it.'

'Childbirth class? Oh yeah. I haven't booked it yet. I don't have much time. There's too much stuff happening at school.'

'Make time. It's not just for you. It's for your baby.'

Nancy thinks about it. Maybe she will, maybe she won't.

DISPOSSESSION

How could they do it? Fern wondered it then. She wonders it now, all over again.

The nerve! Selling her little house, moving her things out without her permission. Surely it couldn't be legal. It shouldn't be anyway. Putting all her possessions in storage. If they did keep them all, if they didn't throw anything out.

Her daughters snooping through all her things. Stacks of old letters, tied up with ribbons. Surely they wouldn't have read them! Her drawers of pathetic underwear: the ripped lace on old nightgowns, frayed underpants with stretched elastic. She can imagine their smirky faces, the way they'd laugh. The hundred-dollar bill hidden beneath handkerchiefs, escape money she'd kept hidden throughout her marriage: did they spend it? Looking through her bank book and cheque book, all her private papers. They had no right!

Sweet little folded C-note. How many years had she kept it? Throughout most of her marriage to Walter. How long ago did he leave? Twenty years? Thirty? She can't remember.

One hundred dollars. A taxi ride to the bus station, and a tip for the taxi driver, then she'd see how far she could travel with the rest. Not far enough. All the same the pretty bill always made her feel free, less vulnerable, as though she had options.

'Brats!' she hollers, 'Rotten brats! God damn you! Hell fire's too good for you!' until the nurses come running and jab a needle into her arm.

Her daughters bawling. 'Remember?' they say, 'Mother, don't you remember? When you were so sick you signed a power-of-attorney paper. That piece of paper gave us permission. We didn't want to use it, but they told us you wouldn't get better. The doctors said you were getting ready to die.'

They are crying, both twins. Good! So they should. It's been a long time since she could make them bawl. When they were little she could do it whenever she wanted.

Fern's crying too. 'Get me a box of kleenex,' she says. 'At least let me have that.'

Winnie and Willie. Winnifred and Wilhelmina. No wonder they're crying, with names like that. I have a lot to answer for, Fern thinks. Those names are high on the list.

'For heaven's sake,' she says. 'Stop snivelling. You're wasting time. Go find me some place to live. Get all my things and put them inside it. Hurry up. Get a move on.'

But her daughters keep crying.

Fern has stopped though. She knows the perfect way to get even. Get their names out of her will. Leave her possessions to a shelter for abandoned kittens or puppies or ferrets. A home for unloved mothers. Does such a place exist? It should.

'Stop that,' she says. 'It's over. It doesn't matter.' Fern has always been able to lie.

She pretended it didn't hurt when her father strapped her bare bottom, too proud to let him see her cry. She learned to move outside herself and watch from far away.

She pretended Walter didn't hurt her in bed, but it wasn't enough. She was supposed to pretend she enjoyed it. 'How was it?' he kept asking. 'How was it?' Until finally, the last time, she told him and he didn't believe her. Lies were safer than telling the truth.

Fern went to rehab while the twins found her an apartment.

LETTERS FROM SARAH

Dear Fern,

People can't be in love and do anything else well. I tried to avoid falling for Martin, intended to turn back at each step along the way. I never wanted to use that 'love' word, or make a commitment, certainly not move in together. Because I'd seen my friends take all those steps, then watched their lives deteriorate. They changed into other people. They didn't maintain their own interests, keep up friendships, concentrate on careers, until eventually, inevitably, their love affair ended and huge blocks of time suddenly became available again. Then I watched them pathetically trying to gather up the scattered remnants of their former lives.

I'd filled in a magazine quiz, listing all the positive and negative aspects of getting into a relationship with Martin, or anyone. But there seemed to be more pluses at the time.

Positive: lots of sex, we'd be able to relax, become more and more at ease, learn what we both enjoy, how to please each other. But there's also a negative side: sexual tension and frustration unless I'm able to communicate what I like, and he's not threatened by my doing so. Masturbation may be lonely, but it works. Not emotionally satisfying, but at least physically. The dilemma of greed, of wanting both.

Positive: intellectually stimulating companionship. But also negative: he doesn't enjoy free-wheeling discussions, prefers to tell me what to think. I always loved high-school debating, defending this side, defending that. Martin considers this argumentative.

Positive: someone to go places with. But I wasn't crazy about his booze-hound buddies, their bloodlust yells while watching hockey and football, their references to broads, their off-colour jokes. He calls my friends artsy-fartsy, refers to the women as lezzies, the men as queers. As if it would bother me if they were.

Now I suddenly realize he'd been jealous of my friends. Too late. I wish I'd seen it at the time.

Positive: he'd be available. But I would grow to expect it. And then worry if he wasn't. Where could he be? With another woman? How could I trust him? I'd become more insecure. Better to jog with a dog instead of a lover. It stays around, is always a comfort, undemanding, accepting whatever crumbs of affection are offered. No need to mend fences: if I say this, how will Rover take it? A dog's not much, but it might be enough.

Other things I didn't notice until later: he's a night person, I'm a morning. He keeps the radio tuned to a middle-of-the-road station. Muzak. I kept switching it over to jazz. I used to tell him easy listening is spelled EEZZZZY, all those Zs standing for snores.

I fell in love with Martin anyway, despite myself. 'This is so good,' we kept telling each other at first, wondering why we'd put it off for so long. Laughing, 'What in the world were we afraid of?'

Martin left emotionally anyway. All men do, sooner or later. I knew this, had read books, was aware what happens next: at first the woman pretends she doesn't care, and sooner or later she really doesn't. I kept waiting to stop caring about Martin.

What is it about men? Are they ever there emotionally in the first place, or just acting out some role they think women expect? Are they simply playing a game? Maybe. Because of course I'd been playing one too.

Finally I'd cried enough. Tears were over; distancing began.

I no longer noticed what time he came home. Just as well. It got later and later. I didn't watch the clock any more, listen for his key in the door, or even look up. Eventually he'd say something, 'Hi. What are you doing?'

'Reading. You home already?'

Cocooned inside piles of books, a fascinating world all around me, one I'd always taken for granted. Library books stacked everywhere, history, geography, science, thick textbooks with footnotes, and references at the back, which sent me back to the library again, following up, searching for more information.

One Saturday morning I left him a note: 'Took the car. Be back for supper.' I just drove around, needing time alone. But all day his mind went crazy, picturing me with a lover, obsessing about it, wondering who he was, what he looked like, imagining our antics in bed, playful at first, and then frantic. Thinking about the guys in the office, one after another, wondering which one I was with, trying to remember what he knew about their sex lives, the gossip and innuendo.

When I got home to make supper he was already there. 'How come?' I asked, 'I thought you were going to the Jays game,' but Martin started right in, 'Where were you? Who is he?' Finally he hit me. It had never happened before, but I suddenly realized I'd always been half-expecting it, and wasn't surprised. Somehow I felt I deserved it.

TROJAN WOMEN

Nancy has been thinking about pregnancy prevention. 'Wasn't there some old Greek play about women who wouldn't sleep with their husbands any more?' she asks.

'Lysistra,' Fern says, getting it wrong. 'But they weren't thinking of it as contraception.'

'All the same, it sure would work.'

'Of course. Abstinence. The only sure method.'

'Books and articles on contraception always recommend it first, but then go on to describe all the other methods.'

'They know there's no chance of it catching on.'

'It will for me. I never intend to sleep with a guy again. Not Brad. Not anyone.'

REHAB

Fern remembers that damn room at the rehab hospital, even though she doesn't want to.

A room-mate got there first. Her pastel posters with flowery verses are fastened to the walls with masking tape. A china plate is propped on the table between their beds:

> To Mother
> Your sun lights up the sky
> until the dark clouds disappear.

Fern reads it aloud, her voice sing-song, sarcastic. 'You'd better keep this somewhere else. I'm liable to knock it on the floor. My daughters would choke before they'd buy me a plate with a mushy message like that.'

'And that stupid poster over my bed.' Fern complains. '*Sunlight shines brightest at home.* Words bumping together but saying nothing. What in the world is it mumbling about?'

'Home's a nice place.'

'Maybe yours was.' Fern mutters. 'Anyway, we're certainly not at home now.'

A plaque shaped like a valentine beside the window: *Love is a cheerful heart.*

'Hallmark nonsense,' Fern sniffs.

She knows the words she wants above her head, a Papago

woman's death song. She tries to remember it. Something about darkness coming toward her...

CHILDBIRTH CLASS

Young couples arrive with blankets and pillows. They've attended a couple of sessions already and know what to do. The women get down on the floor and practise something. Resting, it looks like. Breathing, the instructor calls it. Fern and Nancy watch in amazement. 'Forget it,' Nancy tells the instructor, 'I already know how to breathe. I've been doing it all my life. Anyway if I forget I've got a library card and can look it up in a book.'

'Wait just a second.' The instructor rummages through a briefcase, thrusts booklets at Nancy, who ignores her and storms out the door. Fern takes them instead.

'My name and phone number are stamped on each brochure,' the woman says. 'Please encourage her to call me. She doesn't have to come to the classes. I'll see her alone.'

REHAB MEMORIES AGAIN

Five a.m. Birds twitter as the sky lightens. Fern hears a scampering in the hall. The cat chasing a mouse and maybe caught it. Good.

From the next room the squeak of Mr. Higgins' bedsprings, a steady rhythm. Fern grits her teeth. 'Hurry up, you old fool,' she mutters, 'or I'll come in there and help you.' She laughs, a throaty quavery gasping sound.

Wouldn't that give my room-mate something new to bump her gums about. Instead of going on and on about the past, the folks she went to school with, or lived next door to, or married, or didn't but could have if she'd just crooked her little finger. Always pontificating, 'Those were the good old days. Elders were respected. Men opened doors for women. Children knew their place, were seen but not heard.'

The good old days, my bunioned foot, thinks Fern who still has most of her marbles and can remember what those times were like.

She remembers some old article from a women's magazine: Question: how do you tell a woman from a man? Answer: women are the ones who feel guilty.

Of course they do, Fern thinks. Even though they're always exhausted, from cooking and cleaning, being pregnant, tending babies, washing clothes. They do everything yet still feel guilty, because they know they should be doing so much more. Women know it's their fault when anything goes wrong. They hear of disasters in far-flung countries and wonder what they could have done to prevent them.

Fern is a young woman when she reads that article. Life won't be like that for me, she thinks. It was okay for my mother but not for me. Things will be different.

Her daughters probably think the same thing.

'I need a newspaper clipping,' she tells them. 'The Papago one. Owl Woman's Death Song. I can't remember the words.'

'But everything's packed away in boxes.'

'Didn't you label them?'

'Well, yes, but...'

'It was in the top drawer of my sewing table. A Papago woman's chant.'

The twins stay a bit longer, but Fern is trying to remember the words of the song and ignores them.

DEATH CHANT

Fern finally relaxes, Owl Woman's Death Song fastened to the wall beside her bed:

In the great night my heart will go out,
Toward me the darkness comes rattling,
In the great night my heart will go out.

Fern chants herself to sleep each night and is always surprised
to wake up next morning and realize she's still alive.

MORE PHONE CALLS

Nancy's mother calls Fern every week or so, while Nancy's at
school, checking up, 'Is Nancy all right?'

Fern always starts out rude but gradually forces herself to
become more pleasant. She doesn't want to make things even worse.
When she's gone Nancy will need her mother to lean on. Fern
intends to stay around as long as she can, but she can feel her
strength giving out.

Once in a while the timing's off and Nancy answers and
hollers, 'This is your slut daughter. Go away,' then slams down the
receiver.

LETTERS FROM SARAH

Dear Fern,

What did I expect? We didn't even like the same
music. I had to play my jazz tapes when he wasn't around.
Also Pete Seeger; the union songs and left-wing politics
incensed him. How could I have dreamed we had anything
in common? He couldn't stand Leonard Cohen either,
didn't even know who Stan Rogers was. 'You must have
heard of him. "North-west Passage," "The Mary Ellen
Clark"...' I tried singing a few bars, '"We rise again..."' He
shook his head.

I calculated backwards, the plane crash, Rogers dead
in '84. What was Martin doing at the time? Traipsing

around Europe maybe? Certainly not paying attention to Canadian news stories.

But all the same, Martin, staunch Canadian, who taps along with Stompin' Tom, how could he have missed Stan Rogers? How could I have let it happen? I'm a woman, after all, and assume responsibility for all the lapses and lacks of the world. One female after another, ever since Eve. Now it's my turn.

Of course I didn't know Martin in '84. Some other female was responsible then. But how come I never noticed this incompatibility early on? Why did I become involved with him in the first place?

I tried again, "'Lighthouse Keeper?'"

'Nope.'

How can one ever know what items of significance are missing from someone else's memory bank? I discovered this one by accident.

Dear Fern,

Life is a long series of goodbyes. 'Goodbye, hello,' sing the Beatles and everyone. Probably you knew this already. I am just now figuring it out.

I browse though books in the library, rereading ones I've known before. Time passes but the words never change. Prufrock is still yattering about peaches.

Dear Fern,

I'm fed up with gum disease, fed up with being at an age when dentists worry about my gums instead of my teeth.

My gums are swollen. They bulge in little ridges along the edges of my teeth. They are trying to tell me something: look after us! Pay attention!

I'm fed up with having to look after them and everything.

I try to distract myself by thinking of something else. Staring in the bathroom mirror counting grey hairs: twenty-seven. Too many to pull out. No comfort there.

I'm sick of having to look after everything. Sick of being a woman. Being a caring person has lost most of its charm.

Ignore all this whining. I've never looked after anyone but myself.

BIRTH DREAM, CHRYSALIS DREAM

Dream-time. Nancy glances upward. The sky is so festive. Clouds look like condoms filled with helium, floating around, bumping against each other, plop, a soft balloon sound.

Nancy is travelling in slow motion, on snake time, moving sideways to escape notice, beneath a cover of leaves and underbrush. The feel of grit and stones beneath her, solid things, substantial. Nothing else matters in the world.

Her past life has been so boring and repetitious, her skin toughening, becoming less sensitive, no longer thrilling to the feel of the world she's travelling through.

The old dried-up body that confines her: it's time to let go, shed it, wriggle free.

And she does. She is a moth or butterfly, shedding that old skin, the used-up chrysalis. She is free at last, and moving forward, onward. She is no one, anonymous.

Above her, beyond the clouds, the empty sky is blue or else it's grey, it doesn't matter. Colour has no meaning. Nancy can travel through it. Her trembling wings become stronger, surer.

Until she wakes up, belly bloated and itching. If only shedding were so easy.

APARTMENT

Fern is remembering the hospital again.

'Don't you remember?' the twins keep asking over and over. They show her the piece of paper, official-looking: Power of Attorney. Her signature so awkward she can't even read it. She was probably half-asleep, doped up on drugs. It's so unfair. There ought to be a law, she thinks. Probably there is.

Forget it, Fern tells herself. Forget it and move on. It's good advice. Maybe some day she'll take it.

Anyway she likes her little apartment. A change is nice, though she'd never admit it to the twins. All those possessions piled up over the years becoming more and more oppressive. It began to seem as though they owned her instead of the other way around. This move forces her to go through cartons and make decisions: what to keep, what to discard.

The twins shoved all her furniture into place, left labelled cartons lined along the walls, reluctantly, because the twins really wanted to unpack them. Fern refused, 'Absolutely not! These things are mine!' She wanted to poke through things slowly, reminiscing as she went. The girls kept insisting, but for once Fern had her way. Good, she thinks now, remembering. I'm getting stronger.

It's been months now. Fern's still working her way through those boxes.

Some of her things seem to be missing, but it doesn't matter, she still has way too much. Fern takes her time, waste-basket handy, puttering, sorting through junk and treasures, trying to decide which is which. It's high time she got rid of old stuff anyway, fuzzy snapshots of ancestors she can't remember, old birthday cards from Walter, letters the girls sent from summer camp, Valentine's cards they made in grade school: red hearts on white construction paper.

In the middle of the night she wakens to go to the bathroom, then stays up until morning. What difference does it make what time it is? She can sleep or stay awake, whichever she wants. Sometimes Nancy joins her, making a pot of herbal tea.

Fern sits at the kitchen table ripping up one piece of paper after another, then searches through the apartment wondering what else she can get rid of. There should be an established pattern for this kind of thing, she thinks. An order people should follow. Ritual destruction of the past.

If she still had any friends, every time someone came to visit Fern could give away her books and knick-knacks, but they're all in nursing homes or dead already. Fern tosses things into plastic bags instead. Unless Nancy trundles them off to Goodwill or the Salvation Army Fern drags them to the dumpster behind the building to get hauled away as trash.

Fern wants to get rid of her possessions and simplify her life. Perhaps, once she has done this she'll be able to figure it out. There must be something solid inside her, some essential central core. Maybe if she looks hard enough she'll find it, like a sculptor with knives and chisels, searching for the secret perfect design hidden deep inside a chunk of granite.

December

GET-WELL CARDS

Fern remembers that hospital time again.

Nurses stand get-well cards at attention on the bedside table so visitors have something to look at. They read the messages and signatures aloud. It seems almost like conversation.

Church elders take turns visiting, also a few neighbours, even her daughters. They tiptoe, voices hushed. 'You look fine,' they tell her, amazed, sounding almost disappointed. Apparently she's going to be all right, won't kick the milk can over after all. Not this time, not yet, false alarm.

Time goes on. Visitors bring news from beyond the puke-green walls. They chitchat of trivia, this and that, expecting Fern to feign interest in the useless details of their lives.

They hand Fern flowers, swaddled in cones of pastel paper, carnations or gladioli, already wilting, and then wait for her to thank them, expecting her to be grateful for this chance to watch flowers fade and droop and die. No one thinks to bring a fern, or even an ivy or jade plant, something that will keep growing. Maybe they don't expect her to be around long enough to watch it.

Finally they leave, their goodbyes always awkward, probably feeling the visit has been a waste of time, what was the big fuss about anyway, Fern looks all right. They could have been doing something else instead, anything, nothing, watching TV game shows or ball games or movies, strolling a mall or boardwalk, drinking a cappuccino or latte at some trendy downtown café. Whatever. The ritual acts of urban life.

Fern feels she has failed them somehow, has been found wanting once again, was supposed to act out the old hospital ritual engrained in history. All those paintings of death-bed scenes, family members drooping, draped like quilts around the bedside.

But the visits are useful, reminding the visitors to be thankful for their own good health. They feel a bit smug about it, certain they'll never be old like her, will be always young and vital. A few grey hairs, maybe, or a tinge of pink upon the toothbrush, nothing more. Fern knows. She remembers visiting old sick people and feeling the same way herself.

Ponce de Leon's elusive fountain of youth. Folks keep right on with the search.

FLIGHT

Nancy wanders along Danforth, reading aloud the signs in store windows, looking for ones that say, Part-time Help Wanted.

On the bulletin board outside a Mennonite church she sees a message:

Following Christ is like flying.

You stop.

You drop.

Nancy remembers flying with Fern in that little plane. She'd like to fly a lot farther right now. Escape, the way Sarah's doing. Forget everything: Brad, the pregnancy, her parents. Even Fern.

No. Maybe not Fern.

During migration butterflies soar on thermals to conserve energy. Otherwise they'd never make it. Nancy wants to discover some crutch like that.

GET-WELL CARDS AGAIN

The mail arrives. Bills and junk mail. But Fern is remembering get-well cards.

Fern's visitors want to be helpful, to talk and entertain her. They expect her to just lie there and be quiet, but no such luck. Her tongue still works, the cancer lodged nowhere near her voice-box, her vocal cords, whatever apparatus allows the carrying on of conversation.

'No,' the doctors keep insisting. 'It isn't cancer. Diverticulitis. A bowel problem. Just follow this diet and you shouldn't have too much trouble.'

As if they assume Fern will believe them. She knows doctors tell lies about cancers they can't cure. 'Remember remission?' she reminds them. 'Last week you said I was in remission. It's my body. My life.' She is hollering at them now. 'I'm entitled to know the truth.'

Probably her daughters have asked them to lie.

Fern pictures the cancer, lurking inside her, not as a crab, a cartoon astrological sign, but a hungry black-widow spider, hiding in shadows, behind folds of intestine, darting this way and that, always busy, spinning its intricate instinctive web, stretching threads from one tissue to another, gathering in a bit of omentum, another organ, whatever it can find. Her womb and ovaries and tubes get tangled together, and all the pretty pink tissues that surround them, the pale luminous loops of small bowel, but still the greedy spider keeps reaching out farther, never satisfied, always wanting more and more. In utter darkness, hidden deep inside her belly, the ugly arachnid continues spinning its endless thread.

Fern's daughters show up at the hospital when she least expects it. It always comes as a surprise, a shock. She wishes they'd make an appointment, give her some warning, check whether she wants them to come or not. She would refuse if she had the chance. Too late now for them to pretend to care.

They're so snoopy, and keep asking questions, old stuff about the past. They bring framed photos they'd removed from her walls, always asking, 'Who is this one? Who is that?' As if it's any of their business. And as if Fern still cares about those ancient ancestors. Or this more recent generation, her progeny, these twin-clone daughters.

'Too late,' she tells them. 'Way too late.'

'Too late? Oh dear,' thinking her memory's shot, she can't remember names to go with the photos. Senile. Alzheimer's, maybe.

Fern knows what they're thinking. Well, so what? 'Too late,' she hollers again. Meaning too late now for them to pay attention to ancestors on her walls or anything else in her life, too late to act as if they've ever really known or cared about her, as if they have any idea who she is or how her mind works.

She yells at them to get out, go back to their own lives, leave her alone. A nurse always has to come with a needle to calm her down. Shut her up, is more like it.

She still remembers how good it felt at the time. It was certainly worth it. Probably she swore at them too, nothing too terrible, 'For god's sake,' maybe, or 'damn.' She was mad enough to use worse words, if she'd been able to think of any. She does regret how loudly she yelled though, now, finally, after all this time, but only because of disturbing all the other patients. Anyway she only regrets it a little.

LETTERS FROM SARAH

Dear Fern,

This job is boring, but it doesn't matter. It's just a temp job. As a temporary worker I can quit whenever I want. Some day soon I'll disappear. I'm finally going to head for Mexico to look for the butterflies. I found an article that told where they stay. I've read all the butterfly books I could get my hands on, even novels with the word in the title. There are so many: *The Butterfly Chair, The Butterfly Plague, The Butterfly Ward*. I hum arias from *Madame Butterfly*. Butterfly this, butterfly that.

Perhaps I will turn into someone else, a stranger. Living in some exotic country might cause this to happen. Living close to the equator, where the sun plops into the surrounding sea, where the full moon rolls across the sky like a ball of mercury, scooping up all the stars in its path.

Maybe I'll find a deserted island to live on. Delusions of Robinson Crusoe. A place whose syllables drip like honey from my tongue: Erewhon, Atlantis, Xanadu.

I might drink Tibetan yak milk, Chinese green tea, sake, the juice of pomegranate and kiwi. I'll eat quince, whatever that is, and chives, pickled alewives, will try every size and shape of pasta: ziti, rigatoni, penne...

Can I do it? Do I dare move away from my health insurance and dental plan? Dare eat a peach? Prufrock again.

Dear Fern,

Now that I'm forty-five I know any age is better. Once I was sixteen and knew exactly the same thing. Because I was small and dark I knew boys preferred tall blondes. I tried to be invisible, and slouched along the sidewalks looking even shorter. I kept my eyes down but somehow observed everyone around me. When I noticed the boy I liked I always crossed the street to avoid him.

Now I look at teenage snapshots and realize I was pretty then. Almost beautiful. How amazing. I wish I'd known. Where did it go?

When I was sixteen I was a knockout. Now I'm forty-five and exaggerate. Actually when I was sixteen I just looked okay.

Dear Fern,

Martin used to say, 'I love you,' and then pause. I kept waiting for the next word, 'but.' He never said it, he didn't have to. My mind supplied it anyway.

Christmas is coming, that terrible season of cheery goodwill. I dread it.

FILE CLERK

Fern's mind drifts more and more. All day she wanders backwards in time, becoming younger, younger, younger. Then Nancy dashes in from school and suddenly Fern is eighty years old again.

Memories with no logic to them. Random. Not arranged in chronological order. Once Fern was a file clerk, and she hates untidy disarray. All the same, some file box inside her mind tips over and old memories tumble everywhere. She tries to gather them up as best she can, jumbled together. She's too tired to sort them out.

Fern's eyes blur. She squeezes them shut, open and shut, trying to clear them. She thinks perhaps she has astigmatism of her mind as well as her eyes, her brain relaxing, slipping out of focus, some old memory replacing whatever is happening right now.

Once Fern had a childhood. Those memories are faded, shaded in sepia, like old snapshots.

Fern's father has a desk and a set of coloured pencils sharpened to fine points. They stand upright in a glass jar, bristling like a pincushion or porcupine. 'Don't touch,' says Poppa, as though they might prick her like sharp needles. He gives her worn-down stubs to draw with instead.

Poppa uses sharp pencils to draw houses and stores and buildings. Modern ones with rounded corners, nothing like the ones Fern sees on the streets around her. Buildings that only happen on the streets inside his mind. Rolls of blueprint paper are propped in the corner, each one fastened with an elastic band. Sometimes Poppa unrolls them and explains the fine white lines: walls, windows, doors, stairways. House bones. Her father draws the skeleton shapes of buildings.

One day he asks Fern questions from a *Reader's Digest* quiz: which colours look good together? Her parents keep smiling at each other, as she answers correctly, one question after another, making them proud. 'Maybe she'll be an artist some day,' Poppa says. Fern never admits she'd already tried the quiz and checked the answers in the back of the magazine. Sometimes it is so easy to make them like her.

The *Reader's Digest* arrives each month, and Fern rips off the brown paper wrapper so she can read it first. Mainly she reads quizzes and jokes and anecdotes. She keeps searching for more ways to please them, but the colour-quiz success never happens again.

PHONE CALL

Fern hangs up the phone. 'That's that,' she says. 'The twins have a couple of weeks' holiday, and are heading to Florida for Christmas.'

'Florida? You mean you won't see them?'

'Florida. Yes. It'll be perfect. The weather's nice there, and golf courses are open all year round. The twins love golf and are pretty good at it. They've had lots of practice.'

'But...'

'Don't fret, Nancy, it's perfect. They'll be surrounded by other people who are free, who don't have families cluttering up their lives. They can go wherever they want. They have no responsibilities to stop them, no clutching husbands, no kids hanging around the fireplace afraid Santa won't remember their chimney.'

'But they'll want to be with you...'

'No parents either. Not really. Walter's dead and I might as well be. I've never been a good mother to them. Oh, I didn't actually neglect them, but a baby-sitter wouldn't have either. I probably loved them, but never knew how to show it. Don't you dare make the same mistakes I did. Cuddle your baby every chance you get. Today they call it bonding, but it's really just another name for love.'

'You can teach me that stuff later. Right now I need to learn how to cook a turkey.'

'It's easy. First you go to the library and find a cook book. Then you come home and drink a glass of wine. I can't remember the rest. Oh yes. Watch out. The butcher hides a paper bag of disgusting bits inside the bird. It's a good idea to take it out.' A long pause, then, 'Or you could always make up with your folks and have dinner at their place.'

'What kind of wine?'

LETTING GO

Fern is learning to let go, of life, of memories, the way a tree releases its leaves so they can travel wherever the wind blows, hither and yon.

It is so tempting to hold on: to Nancy, to the baby she's expecting, to the remaining dusty old knick-knacks still cluttering this cramped apartment. Framed photographs the twins nailed to the apartment walls: Fern's daughters, her dead parents and ex-husband. Walter! Imagine! Why in the world would they imagine she'd still want him looking down on her?

Photos of herself when she was young. These are harder to part with. Reminders of her earlier selves. She's unwilling to give them up, thinking no, I still need them, they are mine, they're who I was.

But now she snatches them from the walls, quickly, before she can change her mind, and smashes them into a carton, hard, so the glass will break, piercing the smiling faces. Goodbye, goodbye.

LETTERS FROM SARAH

Dear Fern,

I've just read a magazine article on male rage and am feeling a lot of rage myself, so apparently testosterone isn't essential, though it certainly helps.

Male rage. One more thing for women to feel guilty about.

This is written for the woman who reads about male rage and feels guilty. She always feels guilty.

She has a young boss at the office. Right up to her retirement he'll refer to her as his girl.

She works at minimum wage all day, then cooks and cleans and launders in the evening. She drops the kids off each morning and picks them up again at six. For entertainment she reads them bedtime stories. At parent-teacher meetings she always discovers she's not doing enough.

When she flops in bed exhausted her husband accuses her of being frigid. She's afraid he might be right.

This is written for that woman.

Her husband thinks that foreplay means only before marriage. She has to lie impassive, he says he doesn't want her acting like a whore. But he insists she have orgasms so she fakes them. When he asks her how it was she's learned to lie. He asked her once to tell him when he was doing what she liked, so she told him and he stopped.

He wants her to be a life-sized glossy of Marilyn Monroe. It's hard without the time or money for the hair-do and the facial and the manicure and the make-up and the clothes. She's the same age as he is but he wants her to look like she's his daughter. She feels guilty that she doesn't.

While she's trying to grow his seed she has to give up sex until she stops spotting, and has to give it up again for six weeks after his child kicks and screams its frantic path out of her belly, then has to give it up again until the venereal infection her hustling husband gave her settles down. While she waits the guy is getting it together somewhere else, and he says when he gets caught, 'Baby, it's different for me. I've got these needs.'

The woman knows it's all her fault. This is written to tell her that it's not.

Dear Fern,

Here's some butterfly trivia from library books.

Monarchs may have been named by English settlers, its colour reminding them about William of Orange. So they say, whoever they are.

Also, psyche means butterfly as well as soul. Did you know that? Aristotle used the word to mean both. Maybe that's why paintings of Psyche always show her with wings.

Books don't talk about what interests me though. That magic moment when an earthbound worm, a caterpillar, wakes up transformed, discovering it has wings, is able to fly. What could that possibly feel like?

To soar above the milkweed plant that had sustained it. To waft from one flower to another, wherever it wanted. That freedom. That new butterfly view of the world.

Dear Fern,

A woman is laughing in the next apartment. Someone must be with her. All alone isn't the way that laughter happens. I just tried and I know.

Perhaps she's watching a sitcom on TV. Not a news report, that's for sure. Not a documentary on starving kids in Ethiopia or Afghanistan or somewhere.

Once I saw someone interview a New York writer named Grace Paley. The interviewer assumed Paley was an optimist, but Paley corrected her, said she was actually a pessimist, but a cheerful one.

Me too. Isn't everyone? We know the world is falling apart, we're sliding downhill on a greased toboggan with our eyes shut. But we're smiling anyway. Why not? We might as well.

I could turn on the television and surf channels, searching for the show she's laughing at, but probably wouldn't find it funny.

Maybe she laughs because she's nervous. Remember the classic Mary Tyler Moore episode when Mary laughed during the funeral of Chuckles the Clown?

People laugh to keep from crying. They laugh until they cry.

Today some guy at work mentioned visiting his father at a nursing home. He visits every evening and has been doing this for years. 'Someone's got to feed him supper,' he said. 'Someone's got to get him up walking. Otherwise he'll develop bedsores and pneumonia.' All of a sudden I started crying and couldn't stop. No one will ever do that for me. No one has ever loved me enough.

Butterflies don't cry of course. They are silent. But apparently there's one in South America that is able to make some kind of sound.

Xmas is almost upon us. Omigod. All that goodwill makes me want to throw up. All that sweetness. Lucky I'm not diabetic.

THAT FRIGID WORD

'Frigid bitch,' is what Walter hollers at her when he leaves.

No, Fern thinks. Don't say that. Just leave. Get out. Good riddance. But don't say those awful words because they'll be hard for me to forget.

Impossible, even.

How to get rid of a bad memory? What can she do? Those words of Walter's, she's got to get rid of them somehow, maybe grind them to dust and burn whatever is left. But it won't help. She remembers a physics law from high school: there is always a residue.

Fern talks to herself in the middle of the night. Out loud, so she can listen. She is trying to make sense of things, figure out her life, what she's been doing, and whether there've ever been any reasons why.

She relives her marriage, angry to be doing this again. Surely living through it once was more than enough.

Walter cheats on her. Maybe he never has an affair. She thinks so, but can't be certain, he never admits it, but there are other kinds of cheating. He never lets Fern inside his life. He works long hours at the office at night and on weekends, or so he says. He doesn't have to. His co-workers don't. Sometimes a neighbour mentions that her husband helps with the dishes, or refuses to, that he always reads their kid the same bedtime story, a favourite from his own childhood, whether the child likes it or not. Chatting about him all the time, casually, her husband this, her husband that.

Fern never mentions Walter. She can't imagine what to say.

Fern cheats too, never lets Walter inside her life either. She gives all her attention to the twins. They demand more, but also less. Physically more, but she is able to short-change them emotionally.

Anyway Walter always acts like he works long hours for her and the kids, maybe even believes it himself. No way though. The kids would prefer his time and attention. Fern tells him and tells him, but Walter ignores anything he doesn't want to hear.

Years later she hears the word workaholic and thinks it's a good descriptor. An addiction, working to try to fill some need inside.

Like her with the girls. Sewing matching outfits, pressing intricate ruffles, fluttering and hovering, living vicariously through them. But of course she is always excluded, they don't need her, they have each other.

Walter works too hard. Fern blames his parents. They'd raised him to think he had to get good marks and be successful for them to love him. But Fern isn't his parent. He doesn't need to buy her affection. She thinks he's had too much of it already.

XMAS COMES AROUND REGARDLESS

The twins drop in on their way to the airport, unexpected, laden with gifts.

'Don't wait for Christmas, Mother. Open them now,' they beg, like little kids.

A box of white chocolates, tins of salted nuts. Foods Fern can't eat. Have they forgotten about her stomach and her heart? She almost asks, but for once manages to hold her tongue.

A giant poinsettia plant that takes up too much space. Fern glares at it. Are they stupid? Don't they realize she'd prefer a fern?

A pendant with Fern's birthstone.

A fuzzy housecoat with matching slippers.

Also a cassette tape, the home-made kind. Fern puts it aside, says, 'I'll play it later. It'll take too long to hear it now.'

'But...' Turquoise Cashmere starts to protest, until Lemon Cashmere pats her shoulder. 'Hush now. It's okay. It's Mother's tape. She can play it whenever she wants.'

Turquoise helps Nancy in the kitchen, making tea, arranging a plate with the cookies that they brought, the shortbreads and marzipan and Christmas cake.

'How are things going? How has Mother been?'

'Good. She seems pretty happy, as far as I can tell. She's got me to worry about a little, and a new baby to look forward to. I finally figured something out. I think maybe she was bored before and needed something new to think about.'

'Mother has always had lots of friends...'

'Not any more. She says they've all died off, or moved to a warmer climate. Or else they've disappeared into nursing homes because of strokes or broken hips.'

'She should go on senior citizen outings and meet some other people.'

'Bridge games? Bingo? Shopping trips to factory outlets? Are you kidding? Fern would hate that sort of thing.'

'Perhaps. But there must be drop-in centres, where seniors just go for a cup of coffee and chat.'

'I'll look around. But Fern's Fern. She does whatever she wants to. Anyway she seems okay. Of course I've never known her any other way.'

After the twins leave Nancy and Fern listen to the cassette. On one side the twins sing Christmas carols, a cappella, their voices sweet and trembling. 'Silent Night,' 'Gentle Mary Laid Her Child,' 'O Little Town of Bethlehem,' 'O Holy Night.' At the end, after 'Away in a Manger,' they holler in unison, 'Merry Christmas, Mother!' On the other side they sing lovely old children's hymns that Nancy remembers from Sunday School: 'Jesus Loves Me,' 'Jesus Bids Us Shine,' 'God Sees the Little Sparrow Fall,' 'When He Cometh.' They finish with 'Amazing Grace,' then, breathless, holler, 'We love you, Mother.'

Fern starts bawling and can't stop. Have they ever told her that before? She doesn't think so. She can't remember.

She plays the tape over and over, a kleenex box handy.

THE 25TH

They celebrate, first of all, by getting up late. 'This is the last Christmas I can sleep in,' Nancy says. 'I'd better enjoy it while I still can. I can't even imagine what next Christmas will be like. I don't think it'll be peaceful and relaxed like this.'

Fern has a carton hidden in her bedroom closet, lots of small soft parcels wrapped up inside. Little undershirts with velcro tabs. sleepers, small flannelette blankets. 'They're called receiving blankets,' Fern says. 'I remember that much.' A little sweater and bonnet set. 'Green,' Fern points out. 'Suitable for either a girl or boy.' A fuzzy crib blanket.

'Wow! Look at all this! Am I really going to need all this stuff? Guess I'd better buy a crib to go with the blanket.'

'Not right away,' Fern says. 'I'll empty out one of the top drawers of my dresser. It'll be just the right size. They work just fine.'

'How'd you get all this stuff? Did you go shopping on your own?'

'No. It was a lot easier than that. I phoned the Bay and had them deliver.'

Nancy spreads everything out on the coffee table. She keeps staring. She's grateful, of course, but not sure whether she's happy or not. The tiny outfits make the baby seem too real.

Fern doesn't seem to notice. Nancy gave her a notepad and a set of watercolour pens and she is fooling around with the colours, dabbling, layering one on top of the other, feeling she's probably breaking all the rules about painting, but so what? Surely at eighty she's allowed to do whatever she wants.

Nancy cooks chicken breasts for Christmas dinner, and stove-top stuffing to go with them. She mashes potatoes, and boils frozen peas for a touch of colour. For dessert she serves ice cream with strawberry jam on top. It's the fanciest meal she has ever prepared.

'We forgot to get wine,' Fern says. 'It would have been festive. I should have remembered.'

'Next year,' Nancy says. 'I can't drink right now because of the baby.'

Next year. Fern thinks about it. twelve whole months, 365 days. It exhausts her to think about it. She doesn't want to be around. 'Time to phone your folks,' she says, but Nancy won't. She doesn't intend to spoil this beautiful day.

'Okay,' says Fern, 'but promise me...' Then she stops, not knowing what should come next.

'Promise what?'

'You need someone. Some older woman who's been there before. Not to do anything, just to be there. If I'm not here you'll need your mother. I can't stay around forever, Nancy. I'm just too tired. Promise you'll make up with your mother when I'm gone.'

'No. I mean, yes, I promise. But no. I won't need to. You're here. That's enough. You're all I'll ever need.'

Fern sighs. It'll have to do.

She does phone her daughters though, and tries to tell them how much she loves the tape, that she cries every time she listens to it. She is crying right now as she tells them.

Nancy is listening, pretending not to. She is holding her breath.

1996

January

Dear Fern,

A sweet young couple lives downstairs.

Memory is so selective. I'd almost forgotten what love is like at the beginning, that fascination, the insatiable getting-acquainted time. Holding on to each other. Talking non-stop, because there are so many missing gaps to fill in: everything, all the memories from childhood and the teen years, puppy loves and serious ones, the reasons those earlier relationships broke off. Having sex with your eyes wide open, not wanting to miss anything. Inhaling each other's breath, your juices mingling. That need to enclose the other, never let go, not knowing where one leaves off and the other begins. That intensity.

The opposite of religion, that old caution preached from the pulpit: deferred gratification. Preachers warning folks to defer and to defer and to defer. Wait for bliss to take place in some afterlife; don't grab happiness right now.

Someone to take a shower with, someone to scrub your back. Thinking I'll never have to do anything alone again. The underlying assumption: I'll never want to.

Now what I mainly remember is how love ends, that slow relentless erosion. One day you wake up, open your eyes, and suddenly notice there's nothing left.

Dear Fern,

It has been snowing every day. Where have all the colours gone?

I've turned into a grey woman. I wander through flurries and am invisible. But it doesn't matter. At night I change into a butterfly and glide inside wild technicolour dreams.

Dear Fern,

In the library I found some info about that butterfly place in California on the Monterey Peninsula near San Francisco. Pacific Grove, but it calls itself Butterfly Town, USA.

All the butterflies west of the Rockies migrate there. Eucalyptus trees bloom all winter, providing sweet nectar as well as shelter.

Every October there's a butterfly parade, children in costumes celebrating, welcoming them back. Isn't that lovely? I can't believe this really happens nowadays. It sounds like something that might have happened in olden times: Cree welcoming the return of the deer, Plains indians greeting the buffalo herds, Haida honouring the totem of a clan: raven or killer whale or grizzly bear.

Motorists have to obey BUTTERFLY CROSSING signs. Pedestrians have to watch where they step.

The poor monarchs east of the Rockies have to migrate a whole lot farther, all the way to Mexico. For years scientists wondered where they went. That wintering ground in Mexico wasn't discovered until the mid-seventies by a professor at the University of Toronto. A Canadian! Imagine!

Isn't it amazing that butterflies can travel that far? Apparently they soar on thermals, but even so! 3,000 kilometers!

Mexico is a long way off for me too. But our butter-flies go there, so that's the place I intend to visit. Not today, but some day soon. Very. Fly all the way to Mexico, as close as I can come to butterfly flight.

Dear Fern,

A woman in an apartment across the courtyard does the same thing every day. She eats breakfast on her balcony as though it's summer and she belongs there. Like a child having imaginary picnics in a corner of a back yard, while pretending she's somewhere else. Anywhere.

Here it is, New Year's Day, January already, and she's out there anyway, all bundled up in a coat, scarf, mittens, a blanket over her lap. Perhaps she'll do this all winter long. In TB sanatoria in the old days they believed in the healing properties of fresh air. Patients were bundled up in blankets and placed out in the sun, even in winter. Perhaps the woman across the courtyard has tuberculosis herself, and is trying that outdoor therapy.

She drinks orange juice. Perhaps she has squeezed the oranges herself. Is she remembering orange blossoms, wedding rings, promises made against all logic? Or does she daydream of Florida orange groves, a sign fastened to the gate: PICK THEM YOURSELF, and of course she does, thinking this is amazing, so exotic, something I could never do back home in southern Ontario, in predictable prosaic London.

Toast and jam, a pill (a vitamin maybe?), a thermos of coffee. She pretends to read the morning paper.

I think she daydreams all day long.

She watches other people leave for work, to live their separate lives. Perhaps her husband and children do this. Curving around a corner of her mind, becoming small and smaller. Then with the click of an off-switch, suddenly they disappear.

Perhaps she waits for a phone call from her lover.

I watch her, try to pretend I envy her uncomplicated life, as though my own is more exciting. The poor boring lonesome soul, I tell myself. You really have to feel sorry for her.

Eventually, mid-afternoon, she gets up, gathers her dishes, disappears inside the balcony door, and closes her blinds.

Perhaps she begins writing a letter that begins:

A woman across the courtyard does the same thing each day. She watches me out her window...

PEACHES

'Hey, Fern. It's a nice day. Cold, but bright and sunny. Want to go on another cemetery visit? We could just cruise around, staying in the car, warm as June bugs.'

Fern ignores her, so Nancy asks again, louder this time. Fern glares at her. 'Oh, for heaven's sake, leave me alone.'

Nancy grabs her coat and stomps out the front door, too late remembering her key has been left inside. No point ringing the doorbell right now. Fern probably wouldn't answer. Nancy heads down to the lobby, reads freebie ads from the supermarkets until she calms down.

Meanwhile Fern's mind embarks on a different journey, wanders backward into some earlier time. Maybe Nancy's pregnancy causes Fern's mind to drift backward to those long-ago days when the twins were babies. Not merely remembering. Reliving.

One baby or the other always slung on Fern's hip, or tugging at her clothing, pulling her hair. Like peaches, she thinks, the soft fuzz skin, the curves and clefts of their small round bodies. So helpless. These poor little burdens, needing Fern to protect them.

Someday men will try to claim them. She thinks of orchards, men on ladders, how they prune, pick, spray— using trees and peaches like they use everything.

Fern doesn't want to be touched either. Not by Walter anyway. Holding, tending both babies involves far more physical contact than she wants. 'Leave me alone,' she tells him. These peaches. She'll have to tend this fruit for twenty years. All she ever wanted were flowers.

Fern wears her bathrobe and bedsocks all day long. All weekend, sometimes all week.

Walter comes home from work each day and asks how the babies are.

'Finally asleep.'

'Maybe I'll just take a peek.'

'No, Walter! Stop! Don't wake them up!'

But he always came back carrying a baby. 'Look who I found. Look who was just lying awake in her crib waiting for someone to come and pick her up.'

'You hold her then,' Fern tells him. 'I've had her enough.' She picks up an old magazine and begins to leaf through it.

But the novelty's already worn off for Walter. He hands the infant over. 'I think she's hungry.'

'There are bottles in the fridge. Stick one in a pan of hot water until it's warm enough. While it's heating up maybe you could change her.'

'Well, okay,' he says, 'so long as she's just wet.'

'Oh for heaven's sake, never mind then,' Fern tells him. She knows small babies are hardly ever just wet.

'How did you do it?' she writes to her mother, but of course it was different. Her mother had one child at a time.

Did she cuddle the twins enough? Of course not. She knows she didn't. She was always exhausted. No wonder they turned to each other for comfort. This made her feel rejected, so she ignored them right back.

She wants to apologize to them, try to explain. Now, finally, all these years later. Maybe, when they come back from Florida, she'll be able to find the right words.

The doorbell rings. Fern waits for Nancy to answer it. The bell keeps ringing, driving her crazy, so finally she opens the door. 'Oh! It's you! I didn't know you'd gone out.'

BABY CLOTHES
Nancy shops at Goodwill and returns with treasures. 'Look at these. I don't think they've ever been used.' She unpacks cuddly sleepers, a cozy blanket, and baby bottles still sealed in the original package. 'Look. Someone must have bought these bottles but never used them. Isn't that strange?'

She keeps expecting Fern to pay attention, to even answer.

And sometimes Fern does, and makes perfect sense. Sometimes her mind's right here inside this apartment. Sometimes she knows it's January and Wednesday and remembers who Nancy is. But often not.

CHILDHOOD
Fern is a child again, so small she can crouch down on the ground and see everything that happens. Green inchworms teeter from one strand of grass to another. Ants hurry to and fro carrying crumbs back to their nests. 'Look,' she says, but her parents don't pay attention, ants and caterpillars not being important. 'Don't touch those nasty cigarette butts,' warns Mommy. 'Don't get your hands dirty.'

Fern asks questions all the time: why this, why that? 'I don't know,' says Grandma. 'Go ask your father.' 'Not right now,' says Poppa, 'I'm reading the newspaper.' 'Why this, Mommy, why that?' 'Oh, shush a minute, child. I've almost got the baby to sleep.' Sometimes her mother remembers later to ask what that question was about, but it's always too late. Fern is already thinking of something else or thinking nothing.

Fern is a child and people tell her what she wants to do. 'You don't want to play inside on such a nice day.' 'You don't want to bang around while the baby's having a sleep.' 'You don't want to splash in puddles and get your clothes all wet.' 'No, Fern. That's nasty. You don't want to put it in your mouth.'

'You don't want to eat any more candy,' says Grandma. 'You don't want another cookie. It'll spoil your supper.' 'You don't want brown sugar on your bread.' 'You don't want ketchup in your milk.' 'You don't want to eat whatever junk you find on the sidewalk, crayons or sand or worms. It'll make you throw up.' Fern wants to eat worms and spiders and then throw up all over Grandma. She wants to eat brown-sugar sandwiches instead of supper. She wants to mix all the foods together, pickles and butter and ice cream and cheese and peas and salt and pepper and then throw the whole mess in the garbage.

Fern is a child and has to go wherever the grown-ups say, good places and bad. 'Hurry up,' they say. 'Don't dawdle.' It's always time for grocery shopping or the drug store or the babysitter's house. Time to visit the doctor or dentist or library.

Time means nothing to Fern. She wants to play or eat or sleep forever, or at least until she gets bored. 'Wake up, sleepyhead. It's morning,' says someone, or, 'Put your toys away now, it's time for bed.'

'Read me a story,' says Fern, and her mother sighs, 'Not again. I just read you one yesterday.' 'Oh please, Mommy,' Fern begs, 'Read me another story anyway. I need more.' She always needs more.

People tell her who she loves. 'Of course you love your baby brother. Lots of other little girls would love to have a sweet little baby brother like that. You're so lucky.'

People tell her who to kiss. Aunts and uncles and grandmas and grandpas. Not strangers on the streetcar or on the bus. 'Don't speak to them, Fern. Ignore them. Look somewhere else. Stare out the window.'

Fern wants to be a grown-up and decide what she wants to eat and who she wants to kiss and love.

And finally it happens.

SOUP

Fern's behaviour is becoming more and more erratic. Nancy never knows what to expect.

'I've made some soup, Fern. Chicken noodle, your favourite. C'mon, sit down at the table and try it.'

Fern allows herself to be led to the table, even dabbles her spoon in the bowl, splashing a little, but never bothers to raise the spoon to her mouth.

'Maybe I could feed you some. Would you like that?'

Fern knocks the spoon out of Nancy's hand, mutters something under her breath.

'What? Sorry. I didn't hear you.'

'Get out! Walter and these bratty twins are trouble enough! Go away! Leave me alone!'

Nancy will be glad when the pastel twins return from Florida, so she can ask them what to do.

MAIDENHAIR

Fern finds someone to spend a life with, and assumes he'll feel the same way back. He'll want to spend all his time with her. They will twine together like ivy, tighter and tighter. Everything else in their lives will fall neatly into place. Automatically.

Maidenhair ferns thrive in a cold climate. Southern maidenhair is known as Venus' hair and is slow-growing at first.

Fern decides who she wants to kiss and love but Donny picks someone else instead.

Fern is old now and wants to control what she remembers. Donny. Her first love. She tries not to think of Walter, but his memory intrudes and defeats her.

Walter's just someone she goes out with for something to do, a distraction to take her mind off Donny. But Walter decides Fern's the one he wants, her parents like him, and that's that. Walter is who Fern gets.

He doesn't help around the house, of course not, but that's okay, Fern doesn't expect it, probably wouldn't welcome it anyway. Fern likes things to be done her way or not at all.

Fern decides what she wants to eat, then has to buy all the ingredients and cook them, and wash the dishes afterward. It turns out her favourite foods are not the same as Walter's. He craves all the foods he grew up on, so gets his mother to write out all those old family recipes.

Fern holds tight to a thought from a plant book: ferns do not flower or bear seeds.

But it turns out Fern is able to conceive. She hadn't expected this. For one thing she feels too young. Mothers are supposed to be matronly and middle-aged and wear flowered cotton aprons.

Fern is nauseated for months and can hardly look at food, but it doesn't matter, she has to cook because Walter is hungry anyway.

Her body changes into someone else's shape and refuses to obey her. Fern wears fuzzy slippers all day long. She forgets she's got them on. After all, she can't see them. She tries to remember when she was able to look at her feet. Her belly bounces before her like a soccer ball; she's afraid someone will kick it.

Finally Fern has her sweet little twin babies. She seems to love them. They seem to be the purpose she has been waiting for all her life. She cooks and vacuums with one hand while jiggling a carriage or balancing a baby against her shoulder. She is tired all the time and stops cooking desserts. 'What's next?' asks Walter after the meat and vegetables are gobbled up. 'What do you mean there's no dessert? My mother always cooked pies and cakes and cobblers.' He thinks this is just another phase of Fern's that will soon be over, but for once Walter is wrong.

Fern's babies grow up into children who put ketchup in their milk and want brown-sugar sandwiches instead of tuna fish, but now Fern has turned into a grown-up who says, 'No.' She says it over and over, staring at the girls as though they were strangers. 'Where do you get such crazy ideas?' she always asks them. 'It must be from your dad's side.' The twins know this isn't meant as a compliment.

Fern envies her daydreamy kids. They flop down on the grass watching grasshoppers and ants and spiders, or watching nothing. Their life is so easy.

Fern grows up, just like she has always intended, but sometimes wishes she was still a little kid.

PHONE CALL

Fern is getting harder and harder to reason with. Nancy phones her mother to ask what to do, but her father gets on the extension and starts to holler. Nancy and her mother both hang up.

Her mother phones later when he's gone out, but Nancy's in the shower and doesn't hear the ring.

Fern does though, and is annoyed. She yanks out the jack.

ANOTHER PACKAGE OF LETTERS FROM SARAH

'Hey, Fern. Look what just came in the mail. More letters from Sarah. Want me to read them to you?'

'No. Go away.'

But Nancy is learning how to handle Fern. She begins reading aloud anyway.

Dear Fern,
    I'm still a romantic, still dreaming of men.

I walk along the twilight streets and conjure them up, gaze at houses with lighted windows and imagine a man who is waiting inside. I need to lay my head beside him, graze my cheek against his unshaved face. His hair is tousled as though he just woke up. I run my fingers through it and tangle it even more. His eyes are flecked with all they've known of sorrow, disappointment, kindness, love, and so much more. I will have to spend the rest of my life trying to understand those eyes. And the dear planes of his face, his angled jaw, the vulnerable neck I tongue kisses against. His hands: I could describe them, not with words, but with my skin. The feel of them against me here and here and here. His body stretches toward me, gives as I give back...

Eventually darkness blinds the windows. Still I keep walking the deserted streets.

I've got a long way to go.

Dear Fern,

I haven't made it to Mexico or California yet, but I visited a butterfly conservatory at Niagara Falls and am enclosing a brochure. It's wonderful. I know you'd love it. Is there anyone who could drive you? It's right on the Niagara Parkway. I think it's open every day.

Maybe next year I'll try growing milkweed on the balcony of my apartment to see if the monarchs will come. Apparently they lay their eggs on young milkweed leaves, one egg per plant. The caterpillar lives there for a couple of weeks, eating and growing, shedding its skin again and again, munching on milkweed leaves and its own out-grown skin. Waste not, want not. Then it fastens itself to the plant, a green chrysalis dangling. After the chrysalis splits open the butterfly rests awhile, then is able to fly. Somehow it knows how to do this.

Wouldn't that be wonderful to watch? What a beautiful bug.

Things are okay, except lately I've been having the same dream over and over, a chalk-dust dream.

I am a child, about ten or eleven years old, banging blackboard brushes against a brick wall. I am proud of being the class monitor, allowed to bring the brushes outside to clean them. It is almost four o'clock, the other students have already gone home. A teacher watches from the classroom window. I see his outline from the schoolyard, but can't make out his face. He waits for me to bring the brushes back to the classroom. It is the last day of school, June twenty-sixth. Somehow I know this. Perhaps I've noticed a calendar on the teacher's desk. The date seems important. June twenty-sixth. An ordinary date. It comes every year. I think something must be missing from the dream. Something more ought to happen. As though an old memory struggles through clouds of chalk dust.

I'm not sure I want to pursue this.

Anyway, guess what? I'm out of here. Migrating to Mexico for a holiday. And after that, who knows? Certainly not me.

'Wow, Fern. Sarah's going to Mexico. Isn't that great?'

Fern glowers. 'Sarah? Who's that? I don't know anyone with that name.'

FRUSTRATED

Fern wants a bit of Walter's attention. It doesn't seem too much to ask, but he's always too tired. Anyway his folks raised him to be aloof. She doesn't want much, just a hand on her shoulder when she feels bad, his arm snuggled around her when they sit on the couch, their bodies nestled together like spoons after they climb into bed. He cringes at Fern's touch, and keeps his distance except during sex. At first she assumes all men are like this.

Probably he does cheat. She thinks so, but how can she really know? She can't phone him at work in the evening because the switchboard closes down at six o'clock.

Their sex life never changes. Every Saturday night after the news, wham bam until Walter's satisfied, then off to sleep.

Him, that is.

At first Fern doesn't even realize she's frustrated. It takes her years to figure it out. She slips out of bed and boils water for tea, starts eating cookies, it doesn't matter what kind. Before she knows it the whole package is gone.

She reads trash novels from the library until she can't stand them any longer, then switches to non-fiction instead. Anything. *Thailand Travels, Bird-house Blueprints, 101 Solitaire Games, Trapping Foxes for Fun and Profit.* Finally she reads a sex book and discovers orgasms. After that she curls up on the chesterfield and masturbates at night.

But Fern doesn't want to make love to herself. She'd like Walter to do it. Spontaneous, so she'll be surprised, not always knowing exactly what will happen next. Finally she tries to show him, to explain what she needs.

'What are you?' he asks. 'Some kind of nympho? A lesbian? Or maybe both? God help me, I've been sleeping with a lezzie nympho! Well, that's that! From now on you can just go and fuck yourself! Don't bother waiting around for me.'

She feels like he has slapped her. No bruises or fractures, so someone might notice and call the police, but it seems like wife-beating all the same. Psychological.

That's the end. Their marriage is over. It was over before. Fern just hadn't realized it.

He never touches her again. Never speaks to her much either. Saturday nights he goes bowling, or somewhere. She finally has enough space in bed, the whole double bed to herself. Walter's in the basement sleeping on the recreation-room couch.

His feelings were hurt. It's taken her all these years to figure that out.

GOOD NEWS

'I'm back, Fern. The doctor says the baby's doing fine and so am I. Great news, eh?'

And this time Fern's fine too. 'That's wonderful,' she says, and plugs in the kettle to make tea and celebrate.

It is beginning to drive Nancy crazy, never knowing how Fern is going to behave.

COLOURS

Fern remembers a purple skirt and bright blue sweater. She wore bright colours when she turned sixty to make herself look younger. At the time she was the kind of woman who cared about things like that.

She wore the purple skirt and pretended to be fifty years old at the time. Somehow, in passing, she would mention her age to strangers at bus stops and the strangers seemed to believe her.

She'd already begun subtracting two years from her age each time the calendar claimed she'd added one on.

Looking back now, this seems like such an intricate puzzle, too complicated for Fern to calculate. How old was this woman five years before the purple skirt and blue sweater? How old was she when she wore them? How old is she now? She would get a pencil and a piece of paper if she had any hope of figuring this out.

Before the time of the purple skirt and blue sweater Fern always wore black. Maybe decorated by a silver pendant or locket, but everything else black. A little basic black all-occasion dress, black sweater and blouse, black T-shirt and skirt...

When she was in her teens she added two years onto her age each birthday. Otherwise she'd never be able to grow up soon enough. At some point her actual age must have been the same as the one she admitted to, but she probably never noticed. Too many other things were on her mind.

Her name, for instance.

When Fern is seventeen and pretending to be older, she falls in love with a boy named Donny Randall. She tells her diary he's a dreamboat. She used words like that at the time, learning them from magazines like *Hollywood Idols* and *Screen Romance*.

Fern writes her first name with Donny's last one over and over, practising to be married. She twines their initials together into a monogram, and intends to embroider the design on pillowcases once she has saved enough money to buy some.

Fern has daydreamed of Donny off and on ever since, wondering what her life might have been like if she'd married him. Sprawled beneath her husband, pretending Donny was thrusting inside her instead, but it didn't work very often, only when Walter was gentle and in a good mood.

Donny reaches deeper and deeper inside her, searching for her very centre. 'Am I there yet?' he asks her. 'Oh yes,' she says, 'oh yes.'

Nancy rushes through the door.

Fern is suddenly an old woman again, wondering, is that really the way it was? Probably not.

MOHAIR

Once Fern was young and lovely and had a boyfriend named Donny Randall. In faded snapshots he still is handsome and Fern looks as lovely as her daughters. She wonders if this could possibly have been true. Certainly people never mentioned she was beautiful at the time.

Fern has read somewhere that you can't go home again, but she keeps trying anyway. Retracing old footsteps, and half-remembered conversations from Sunday dinners. Inhaling the aromas of home baking, trying to find her mother and grandmother inside old kitchens. Uncurling blueprints and wood shavings to find her father.

As she reads fairy tales to her children, she feels the mohair bristles of an old chesterfield prickling her bare legs. That piece of furniture belongs inside a house that was torn down years ago. The tattered sections of an old street map keep unfolding in her mind.

DREAM WORLD, REAL WORLD

Nancy goes for long walks every day. Even though she's eight months pregnant and feels enormous, her doctor insists that walking is good exercise. Anyway, it is something to do.

This time when she returns, Fern is waiting for her, a piece of paper in her hand. 'The mail came, an envelope from someone named Sarah. There was nothing inside it but a piece of paper for you.'

Nancy reads aloud, 'If you see Nancy give her this. It's good advice. *When you're pregnant it's important to dream beautiful dreams when you're asleep...*'

'That's foolish,' Fern says. 'It doesn't make sense. As if you're able to control what you dream about.'

Nancy keeps reading, '*... and when you're awake to think beautiful thoughts.*'

Nancy smiles, because it feels true. She's finding it harder and harder to focus on everyday life, to concentrate on her paperback copy of Dr. Spock. Her world that is dream and her world that is real keep unfolding into each other. She seems to be watching herself from far away. Both worlds are as fleeting as childhood; if she once looks away they'll be gone.

FLU

Fern is sick. Somewhere in her right temple a wild creature rolls over and stretches and breathes too loud. It does this over and over. It nudges against a tender section of her brain. It almost makes her forget the pain in her gut.

Once twins crowded inside Fern's belly and twisted and turned this way and that trying to get comfortable. What is happening inside her temple feels something like that. Fern would say so if she could speak, if she could think right now, if the creature wasn't crowding inside her right temple.

Gifts are lined up on a bedside table: tylenol to make the creature go to sleep, ginger ale to keep her strength up because she refuses anything else. She has to figure out some way to keep the creature from getting any of the ginger ale. If she sips slowly enough perhaps her thirsty throat cells will absorb all the sugar before it reaches the creature in her brain.

Words drift around her, a voice she almost recognizes. Fern is disappearing, almost transparent. She is imaginary, some woman from a storybook or the bible. Delilah, maybe, or the Queen of Sheba. Eve in the garden of Eden, but she doesn't want an apple, just wants someone to refill her empty ginger-ale glass.

Feverish but shivering, Fern manages to be both hot and cold at the same time. She wonders how this could happen. It doesn't make sense. Nothing makes sense any more.

Someone is holding a cool cloth against her forehead. A fevered brow seems beautiful in fiction but unpleasant in the real world. This is the sort of nonsense her mind is able to focus on.

Her body as betrayer.

Someone touches her forehead and says she doesn't have a fever. 'I do so,' she tries to argue, but her words are garbled and of course no one can understand them.

Inside her temple the creature laughs, a long nasty menacing sneer. 'It's so easy to fool doctors,' it mutters, and laughs again.

Voices are gone, voices return. Fern can't discern a pattern.

'Is someone there?' she asks in a fluttery voice she doesn't recognize. Finally she gets up to see, moving slowly, because the creature is finally asleep and she doesn't want to wake it up.

The living-room armchair is beside Fern's bed. Imagine that. And someone is sleeping inside it, curled up under an afghan. Fern peers closer. 'Who are you?' she asks, shaking the sleeper's shoulder. 'Donny Randall? Are you Donny?'

Nancy jumps up startled, 'What? What?'

SUNNYSIDE

Fern is lost inside a memory or a dream. She can't tell them apart any more.

She is seventeen years old and on her way to the Sunnyside amusement park. She is riding on a streetcar, one of the nice old wooden Witt cars with a heater in the middle. A sweet boy she loves sits beside her. Donny offers her a piece of gum. 'No thank you,' says Fern politely. Her mother taught her how to behave like a lady. She sits still, knees clenched tight together.

It is hot. Fern feels perspiration gathering inside her wide straw hat. They eat a picnic lunch beside the lake, drink orange pop. This happens right after the roller-coaster ride.

'I don't feel well,' she tells Donny, meaning, I'm going to throw up, and then she does, with him sitting right beside her, either watching or looking away. It is the most embarrassing moment of her life. Later they walk along the boardwalk and try to pretend it didn't happen. 'This is where they have the Easter Parade,' Fern tells him. 'All the women wear new coats and hats. Coloured ones. Not like the dark clothes they wear all winter. Their pictures are in the newspaper.'

It is so hot. Fern and Donny sit on a bench and watch people walk past. 'We could dance when you feel better,' Donny says.

Dancing. If he puts his arms around her he will notice the smell of vomit. Fern loves him, so has to be careful what she says. 'Mmmm,' she murmurs.

'Or we could ride the merry-go-round and try to catch the golden ring. We can do whatever you want.'

'I don't know. I've got an awful headache.' The bright sunlight hurts her eyes. She rests her head against his shoulder for a moment and falls asleep.

It's dark when she wakes up. The midway shimmers with electric lights. 'My arm fell asleep an hour ago,' Donny tells her.

'Oh no! I'm sorry.'

He tries to kiss her but Fern squirms away. Do I smell of vomit? she wants to know, but is too embarrassed to ask.

'C'mon Fern. I've waited all this time to kiss you. You leaned on my arm until it was numb but I didn't move it. I didn't want to disturb you.'

Fern's mouth tastes awful. She needs to brush her teeth. If Donny kisses her now he will never want to do it again. When they finally do kiss she wants it to be perfect. 'No.' She turns her head away.

Donny takes her home, kisses her hand and leaves. Her hand! The one part of her anatomy where Fern hadn't already imagined his kiss.

He never asks her out again. She meets Walter on the rebound, and that's that.

Fern gets married. Everyone does. Do all the others immediately regret it? She has no idea. No one would ever admit such a thing.

But finally Fern has her babies. She has done what she was supposed to, what everyone expected. She can relax. Suddenly her problems with Walter don't seem all that important.

This is the best part of her life, she thinks. Everything else led up to this moment; whatever follows can be only anticlimax. Her babies so helpless, completely dependent. This symbiosis: them needing her; Fern needing them to need her. Clutching at each other, inhaling each other's breath.

Babies exist. They need to be held. Fern holds them.

They have a father too of course. Walter. He leaves each morning, reappears each evening, eats supper, reports boring details about his day. Fern tries to listen, pretends to care. Each morning he disappears, from her presence, from her mind. Finally one evening he doesn't come back, and Fern hardly notices at first, and then pretends she doesn't care.

Walter. It's been so long. What did he look like? Fern can't remember.

Once he told Fern she was beautiful. Long ago, before she had babies. Maybe he really meant it.

> Ferns are not useful, serve no economic purpose. Their beauty is justification enough. They simply exist, hidden in dark shady places, to be discovered, to be enjoyed.

Maybe she always has been attractive and didn't know it. Because she feels beautiful right now. Peaceful. Serene. Warm sunshine surrounds her. Her soft green fronds gently flutter in the breeze, to and fro, to and fro...

TRAVELLING ON

Nancy calls Fern, 'Hey, guess what? You've got a letter with Mexican stamps. It must be from Sarah. Maybe she's found the butterflies! Rise and shine. Hurry up. Let's see what it says.'

No answer.

'I'm opening it up, Fern. I'm saving you the trouble. Okay, listen. Here's what she says: "Dear Fern. This is bad news. I've remembered the rest of the blackboard story..." Hurry up, Fern. It's hard to holler like this through your door.'

Finally Nancy pushes the bedroom door open a crack. 'Hey, sleepyhead. Sarah must have found the butterflies! Wake up.'

Then, 'NO! OH NO! FERN! COME BACK! PLEASE! DON'T LEAVE ME! I NEED YOU.' Hollering, sobbing, hysterical. 'OH NO! I LOVE YOU! I CAN'T MANAGE WITHOUT YOU! COME BACK HERE! COME BACK!' Falling onto the bed.

Hugging Fern, shaking her, 'You promised you'd be here! You said you'd stay with me! I can't have this baby without you!' Grabbing Fern by the shoulders, trying to make her sit up, but all the time knowing Fern can't hear her. It's too late. Nancy's been abandoned. She's all alone.

Finally Nancy stops crying, picks up the phone. 'Momma?' She tries to control her voice but can't. 'Momma?' Shuddering, hiccupping, her voice high and squeaky like she's a hysterical little kid. 'Quick, Momma! I need you! Fern won't wake up!'

'Give me the address. I'll call 911 and rush right over.'

'Hurry up! I need you now!'

As she's hanging up Nancy hears her momma holler, 'Ross! Start up the car! Nancy needs us quick!'

Nancy runs back to Fern's bedroom, hollers, 'Fern! Fern!' and tries to shake her awake. 'Don't do this to me! Don't go away! I can't raise a baby all by myself!'

She holds Fern tight, can't let go of her yet. She still needs her.

But then she looks at Fern's face. It has been transformed somehow, relaxed into some sweet expression, all the worry lines erased. Almost she could be smiling.

She looks so peaceful and happy, Nancy thinks. She'll be with me always. I have to believe this. Fern would never abandon me. She'd never leave me on my own. She'll hover nearby where she can watch. She'll be close whenever I need her. I can't have this baby otherwise. I won't be able to raise it.

Somewhere a doorbell is ringing. Nancy ignores it.

She yanks Owl Woman's Death Song from the wall, then sits down gently on the edge of the bed. Holding the Papago verse in one hand, Fern's cool hand in the other, Nancy begins to chant over and over, 'In the great night my heart will go out,' sobbing the words at first, hiccupping, her voice shaky, then calming, becoming stronger.

The apartment superintendent unlocks the door, paramedics rush inside carrying boxes of equipment. They reach past Nancy and check Fern's cold body for a heartbeat. When Nancy sees them pull out the paddles she shakes her head. 'No,' she tells them. 'Fern wouldn't want to come back.'

Nancy's father glances in the bedroom door, says, 'We'd better keep out of the way,' but his wife shoves past him, grabs her daughter and holds on tight. 'Nancy, sweetie, it's okay. Nancy, honey. it'll be all right.'

Nancy doesn't stop chanting or look up, just hands over the piece of paper.

And now Nancy and her momma are chanting together, in unison. 'In the great night my heart will go out. Toward me the darkness comes rattling. In the great night...'

This holy moment. They are holding each other, both of them weeping, but chanting anyway.

Fern's face is relaxed, beautiful, serene.

The once worm soars.

MY SINCERE THANKS TO
- the Pulp Press 3-day novel writing contest for prompting the writing of the Bathurst Quay section of the novel
- the Ontario Arts Council Writers Reserve, Macmillan Canada and The Mercury Press
- Guy Uddenberg, Airport Duty Manager, Toronto Island Airport
- Michael Moir, Archivist, and Elene Ftohogiannis, Archives Assistant, The Toronto Harbour Commissioners
- the late Libby Scheier, who, while vacationing, kindly loaned me, almost a stranger, her Bathurst Quay apartment, my introduction to the neighbourhood
- Jane Malyon and the late Ted Plantos for their helpful comments on early versions of the manuscript
- Billy Malyon, then age 11, who suggested that the too-long (10 word) title, which I loved and was committed to, instead become the first sentences of the novel
- Holly Briesmaster whose wonderful butterfly painting appears on the cover
- Bev Daurio, once again editor par excellence

ACKNOWLEDGEMENTS
- Cogswell epigraph: 'Now The Once Worm...' from *With Vision Added*, Borealis Press, 2000. Used by permission of the late Fred Cogswell
- bissett epigraph: 'th melting horizons uv madagaskar,' from *hard 2 beleev*, Talonbooks, 1990. Used by permission of bill bissett
- Chuangtze epigraph: 'On Levelling All Things,' Chuangtze, in *The Wisdom of China and India*, Lin Yutang, ed. New York, Random House, 1942
- Jameson quotation: *Winter Studies and Summer Rambles in Canada*, Anna Brownell Jameson, McClelland & Stewart, 1965
- The Owl Woman chant: quoted in Frances Densmore's *Papago Music*, Bureau of American Ethnology Bulletin No. 90, Smithsonian Institution, Washington, D.C. 1929, p. 126

Background readings that were of particular interest include: information in the Toronto Harbour Commissioners archives; Hoshizaki, Barbara Joe. *Fern Growers Manual*, New York, Knopf, 1975; Brewar, Jo. *Butterflies*, New York, Abrams, 1976; Feltwell, John. *The Natural History of Butterflies*, New York, Facts on File Publications, 1986. Halpern, Sue. *Four Wings and a Prayer*, New York, Knopf, 2001; Lanken, Dane. 'Winged Wonder,' *Canadian Geographic*, May/June 1993.